# THE BLACK WOLF AND THE RED HARE

AUGUSTA GREY

Editorial Services Provided by Amber of Brightline Editing

# CONTENT NOTICE

This book contains scenes of graphic sexual (consensual) acts, violence, blood and abandonment of a child.

# CONTENTS

# MILDRED

*October 3rd, 1556*

Lady Cecil was tired of her human bones.

The night was deep and still over Burghley House, and no soul stirred in the halls. She lay in bed, trying and failing to will her chaotic mind to settle.

Her husband returned from London tomorrow morning, and it filled her with dread. He would bring some new duty with him from the Queen, and more talk of invasion on the Continent.

As always, their son Robert would be caught between the magnetic pull of his father toward the court of the Virgin Queen and the wisdom she could offer him as a mage. Their son was nine, and still enchanted with his budding magic, but that would soon change. The call to serve the Crown was faint, but even she could hear it in her husband's voice when he told stories of court masques and Elizabeth's dazzling beauty.

In a handful of seasons, Mildred's son would leave her to live the life of a man at university, and she would have nothing left but cold stone walls and a taskmaster for a husband.

She stilled her breath and closed her eyes, calling upon the steady magic within her. Mildred released her body like unlacing tight stays. Her soul spilled out from the boundaries of human flesh and rose up through stone, wood, and plaster until the estate unfolded before her.

Someday, when Robert's magical resonance revealed itself, she might teach him how to slip from his body into the night.

Strong winds from the east cleared the star-pricked sky of clouds and freed the half-moon to shine over the gardens, the orchards, and the lord's wood. A speck of black in the sky grew larger until it settled beside her spirit on a chimney, such a loyal bird that it knew its master's mother even in her phantom form.

The raven croaked affectionately at her as she slipped into its mind. Her son called the bird Harry, but it had no name for itself. She brushed the raven's mind gently, and the creature accepted her.

*How is your master?* she asked in the language of beasts.

*He hates his father; he loves his father. He loves you; he hates you.* The bird replied with the simple logic of an animal.

All children hate and love in equal, ever shifting measure. Robert was a sensitive child and had not yet grown into the fullness of his emotions. She was pleased that he allowed himself to feel them.

*Keep watch over him tomorrow.* She slipped out of Harry's mind and left the bird to its hunt. His croak followed Mildred into the night as she skimmed through the dark wonderland of the orchard, where small furred creatures darted among the trees on the quest for fallen apples.

Her soul slipped past a stalking tomcat, but his form was

too slow and lazy for her tonight. She wanted something quick and filled with urgency.

Not long after Mildred entered the woods, she found the little body of a red-brown hare. Her essence latched onto it and invaded the animal's form like an illness. Its fragile mind tried to fight her, but it retreated into the furthest reaches of its instinct when the rabbit lost the battle.

*Lepus Europaeus,* the last flickers of her human intellect whispered before the knowing of the hare overtook her.

Mildred was gone. In her place, a quick, clever red hare darted out from her warm burrow and rooted near the entrance, looking for forage.

The night was dark and filled with enormous sounds, but there was no hurry. Each moment flowed into the other as she followed her nose toward a strawberry patch that had not died with the first frost.

Mildred's heart beat at a punishing speed, heating her blood and fur as she navigated the cold dark. The wind shifted, and her heart doubled its pace, pumping her through with delicious, invigorating fear.

She scented a predator in the shadows.

There was enough human left in her to savor the feeling as her rabbit's body stilled, listening for the source of the scent.

There were no words in her small, focused mind to describe what stirred in the dark, only flashes of fur, teeth, and claws.

An ancient memory of short chases and bloody ends.

She must run, but where? The scent shifted with the wind until the agitated energy of her terror built up into a crescendo, and she rushed off into the random dark. Something in the hedgerows behind her took off.

Four heavy paws beat into the wet ground, punctuated by hot panting breath, wet with drool.

*Canis Lupus.*

Surprise jolted Mildred back into human consciousness. There were no wolves in England. Their queen's grandfather had killed the last of them.

The beast was closing in on her, its scent growing stranger the closer it got. It smelled of leather, blood, and wine. A man's scent.

An odd wolf was stalking the estate, less than a mile from where Mildred's body lay in Burghley House, where her son slept.

Some strange magic was at work, and she would not ignore it.

The wolf growled and snapped its teeth in frustration as Mildred outwitted the beast with the mind of a woman in the quick body of a rabbit.

She led him into the Rose Grotto, a folly garden she had built deep in the wood where Mildred could read and spend time among the wild things in her mortal skin. There was a stone bench and a simple fountain fed by a cold well so overgrown with roses that the water tasted of them.

Mildred leaped onto the bench and spun around to face the wolf. The scent of humans must have led him to stop in the center of the clearing.

They locked eyes, black against gray. If Mildred were standing in her own body, she would have screamed. The wolf before her was the size of a pony. The creature was pure black, except for a large white stripe that covered its right eye. It shimmered like silver in the moonlight.

*You will come no closer, wolf.* The rabbit words came loud enough that the other creatures watching their encounter from the shadows scurried away. Mildred's body was small and delicate, but the magic it contained was not to be trifled with.

*I will go where I please, little strawberry.* The wolf's voice rumbled like summer thunder as it stalked the perimeter of the grotto.

*You have a terrible nose. I have had no strawberries this night.* Mildred often wrote down the conversations she had as a beast the day after her skin-walking. It was simple, yet lyrical, like the language of the fae, though some of the charm was diminished as she faced down a magical wolf on her family's lands.

*I scent you perfectly. You smell of summer berries, ripe for fang and claw.* There was a strange hunger in the animal's voice, something base and human that had nothing to do with death.

*Your head will hang over the mantle of Burghley House if you come too close. Leave. This is no hunting ground for you.* The rabbit's body entangled her magic, leaving her defenseless. If her beast voice did not drive him back, then she'd have to abandon the rabbit and return to her own body.

*Come, little strawberry. You wanted a chase, and I will give it to you.* The wolf snapped its teeth and stomped its paws into the ground, clawing and digging a deep track into the wet earth.

Such a chase would end in the rabbit's death and an aching headache for her tomorrow morning.

*I have no time for such nonsense. Leave these lands, or I will send men with hand cannons and swords tomorrow night.* Her curt words had no effect whatsoever on the wolf.

He grinned a fanged grin, tongue lolling out of his mouth as he took in deep, panting breaths.

Then he moved toward her, slowly and controlled and full of deadly intent.

It was time for her to abandon the rabbit to its fate. She hadn't meant to cause the poor creature's death, but there was nothing to do about it now. At least she knew about the unnatural wolf and could do something about it in the light of day.

Just as the wolf lunged for her, Mildred released the rabbit's form and shot up into the night. The echo of cracking bone and tearing fur followed her over the orchard and down through the stone manor until she settled back into her own body.

Lady Cecil did not get much sleep that night. The longing howl of a wolf in the deep wood kept her awake until it retreated back into the shadows shortly before dawn.

# SYMON

"There are two of them." Symon's voice echoed the growl of his wolf. He stumbled into the small, windowless room to find his companion pacing the length of the dirt floor.

He had pushed himself too close to the rising sun and had not returned until the sky shifted from black to blue.

Stefan Orrens, Symon's companion and commanding officer, caught him before he swooned. Stefan was lithe and beautiful, with a warm mouth that was often too generous with his smiles. Sky-blue eyes hardened as Symon slumped against the other vampire. He had to pass the large man from one hand to another to make sure the door latched shut, lest the sun creep into their lair and roast them both as it rose into the sky.

"Two of what?" Stefan asked. He laughed as he settled Symon's shaking, sweat-soaked body on a nearby pallet of hay and wool.

"Precious Ones. Your informant was wrong. There is another. She is the wife of a lord, too." Symon grinned even as his teeth ground together. He had spent a fortnight in his wolf skin, pretending to be Stefan's tamed pet during their channel crossing. Now his flesh had forgotten how to be a man, and it rebelled against him.

"Well, that changes the landscape somewhat," Stefan said. The vampire took his charge of gathering their Precious Ones as serious as the grave and he did not enjoy complications. He was quaestori, a protector of the blood. The only time Symon had ever seen that sunny disposition crack was when a mortal mate might be threatened.

The curse of clan Lupou rode Symon hard as his blood teeth descended and he fought for control of his bones. He had mastered the form of bat and wolf, but not the spider. Symon doubted that his mind would survive drawing in the alien intelligence of a spider skin, the form of the wolf was hard enough to detach from his human mind.

*The heart of a wolf cannot break. It knows nothing but instinct and pursuit.*

Symon writhed on the thin pallet of human rags and faced his shattered heart. The woman he'd taken as his own was long gone, sent to his people's homeland in Wallachia to grow into her new nature. He had given their immortal gift without permission from Centurion Yasha Darkov, and he had done so in the midst of war.

Yasha was soon to be made High Commander of the first Legion and it did not bode well that Symon had disgraced himself under Darkov's direct command. It was too easy to lay with a mortal and make them a vampire. Symon had not been the first to disgrace his cohort with lust, but he had done so without shame.

He was lucky that his punishment had been so light.

His elders said that two vampires could not stoke passion between one another, but Symon would try for Amaranth. He'd taken her as a mortal woman, and he longed to help her explore her new senses.

Instead, Darkov had sent him from the front lines in Flanders to accompany the Glasul Stefan Orrens to England as nothing more than a guard dog, with his rank stripped and his sire dishonored. Symon would not partake in the spoils or the glory of dismantling the Holy Roman Empire or France.

His fate was to support Stefan's glorified kidnapping. The council was full of shite. There was no honor in leading mortals into Terra Noxa with trickery or outright abduction.

Symon was a wretched sack of bones and flesh, sweating like a human on his deathbed while his companion paced across the hard-packed dirt floor of their meager lodgings.

"Calm yourself, Glasul. We can handle two pretty mates between us,"Symon said.

It was unseemly to make such base jokes about their most precious, but Symon was a base thing, a beast who would soon forget what it was to walk and speak like a man.

Stefan, as a Glasul, was too attached to what remained of his mortality. Even now, Stefan paced, and sighed and smiled like a human; taking pains to move as one so as not to alarm his Precious Ones. Glasul had magic and the intelligence to wield it but they'd lost their instincts.

Balaur like Yasha Darkov had not lost their inner beast and yet they managed a discipline Symon could never match. He wondered sometimes when the three clans would finally go to war against one another; would it be after their crusade of blood across Europe?

Symon's mind was fractured; half beast half man. His thoughts came like fevers.

When this business was over, Symon would shift back into his fur and disappear into the forests of the Rhineland. There was nothing left of his black mortal heart after Amaranth. Terra Noxa could continue her fight; against the mortal kingdoms or one another.

"Disrespectful dog." There was no bite in Stefan's words. The fresh-faced vampire sat down next to Symon's bedside and shoved a cup of blood wine into his shaking hands.

"There's no need to bring old clan animosities into it. We are on the same side. It is in our best interest as kin to work together in the great hunt," Stefan said in that infuriating tone that managed to be serious and charming at the same time.

Symon had never known another vampire as singularly focused on their mortal liabilities, but Symon was much too jaded from his long centuries without sexual companionship to believe the chivalric lie.

"You romanticize the bond like the others, and yet you call it the hunt. Does that not go counter to your chivalrous intentions?" Symon said.

Let the Glasul play at being human with their spells and the Balaur channel their nature into the heat of battle. Symon was Lupou; his kind was closest to the true beast that dwelled within the vampire.

He knew well how beasts mated. It was not polite or genteel, or sane.

"Your long teeth are showing, grandmother," Stefan said with a cherubs grin. Damn Stefan Orrens; if nothing else, he was an amusing monster.

"The better to eat up little strawberries," Symon mused, laughing at his own joke. The mage woman intrigued him. He had sensed that she was one of their rare-bloods, but there was so much more to that brave little rabbit. He couldn't help but wonder what she looked like in her human skin, or how that skin would taste on his tongue.

"Enough of your lewd musings. Now tell me, what did you find on the Burghley estate?" Stefan's network of spies suggested that there was a young peasant woman who could have the trait, but Symon had sensed it in the earth elemest in the lord's woods that evening, too.

"I believe Lady Burghley came across my wolf. She used the language of beasts and inhabited the body of a rabbit, but I scented her ripeness," Symon said. His teeth itched and his mouth watered, yet there was no true scent to pair with the woman. "She is one of ours, but we must continue our investigation. There is talk of witchcraft in the villages, and the peasant will soon be accused."

Even he saw the stupidity of English law. Like their continental kin, the mortals who ruled Britain embraced their noble mages but persecuted lowborn witches. They shared the same power, but not the same freedoms.

"Then we cannot tarry much longer. Tomorrow night, I will go find the girl, and you shall hunt the lady," Stefan said decidedly.

Symon nodded and forced a long pull of fortifying wine down his throat. It tasted bitter on his tongue, but he had to rest and recover what little self-control he possessed, for tomorrow night he would find his strawberry and pluck her himself.

# MILDRED

"How do you make the oranges grow out of season?" Robert was a clever boy, growing too fast into his ninth year, but Mildred didn't mind answering his questions. It was like discovering magic all over again through him.

"That is an excellent question." She smiled as Robert hopped up onto the pock-marked workbench to get a better view of the orange tree Mildred tended. The feeble autumn light intensified through the thick panes of the hothouse, warming them both as she settled into her lesson for the day.

"Before I answer you, can you tell me what this species of orange is called?" she prompted, waiting patiently as her bone-handled shears sliced off a dying shoot from the healthy trunk.

"Naranja Sanguina, blood orange. Father brought it from Sicily for you."

Pride welled inside her chest. Soon, her boy would be off to Oxford to continue his formal magi training, but for now, they could spend a few more seasons together growing good things in her glass palace.

"Yes, quite right on both accounts." Her pale, slender hands grasped a ripe orange and plucked it easily from the stem. "Oranges need light and heat to thrive, but they can do so without the aid of magic in most places. Our home does not get enough sun, sadly, and even with the help of the glass walls, the tree would soon wither and die once the August sun waned."

Mildred handed the orange to her son, which he took with the same slow patience with which she had taught him to cast his first sigils.

"Then why does our tree grow so strong?"

She lifted a hand toward the tree, and a curling stem followed the motion, lengthening and growing thicker as she guided it up toward the light.

"Our power comes from the earth, and she allows us to borrow life from one place to give it to another." She pointed to the hearty pot of briar roses sitting on a sill behind him. As she drew life from the briar, the orange tree swelled, its dull leaves growing green and fruit ripening before his eyes.

The briar couldn't sustain an entire tree on its own and withered into a drooping, brown echo of itself.

"Are the roses dead?" Her son asked with a curious lilt to his words that made her wary.

This had been the hardest lesson of her young life. Mildred remembered being disturbed for weeks, and she had refused to practice her sigils until her tutor bruised her knuckles with his reed.

Robert took to the concept too readily, and that gave her pause.

"Yes, that is the price. Sometimes we have to choose what to kill and what to cultivate. The briar rose is a common flower and quite hearty, but the orange is rare." Would he understand that sometimes their most sacred and difficult task as mages was to make hard choices?

She hoped he would, that he would somehow differ from her own father and the mages that had come before him in their family. She did not know what resonance her son's magic would chose to take yet; it was taking him longer to specialize than most children.

It was good. Robert would find his calling in time. The heartiest of flowers took their own time to bloom.

"That is a fine, sensible choice." Robert sat up straight, smiling as he used his father's words.

Mildred had hoped that her husband's absence would spare Robert from his influence, but every day, his invisible hold grew stronger.

Of all the things Mildred endured in her marriage, her son was her bright spot, and she felt a wave of icy terror when she realized Lord Burghley would soon steal him from her.

None of this was her son's doing, so she was careful to keep her fear and sorrow out of her voice when she answered him.

"Just so, as your father says." Her smile was brittle, and the sudden coldness of her fingers made it difficult for her to grip the shears.

"What is it I always say, my lady wife?" A voice laced with false fatherly warmth slipped through the open entrance to the greenhouse, and Robert leaped from his perch on the workbench. He launched himself into his father's arms, and Lord Burghley played the part of the doting father like a convincing actor, doling out his calculated charm as he hoisted his son up into a crushing hug.

"Our lesson was about pruning life with magic. Mother is so very clever!" Robert offered the orange to his father as Mildred turned around and carefully arranged her face into the mask of placid openness that her husband expected from her.

She took her time untying her coarse linen overcoat to reveal her crimson velvet gown; transforming from mage to lady with a subtle, demure shift it had taken her over a decade to master.

"She is, and you'll do well to take her lesson to heart. Now run off and start your Latin; Master Cathay will be here soon, and we must not keep our tutors waiting."

Robert grinned and ran off without another look toward his mother, as eager to learn his Latin as most boys were to run wild in the dark wood.

With their son's small footsteps receding into the cold vastness of Burghley House, her husband turned to her, his former self restored.

As cold as a shark, as severe as death.

"Forgive me for intruding unannounced. I do not mean to interfere with the running of the estate, but I have a grave matter to discuss with you." He addressed her the same way he spoke to his clerk or the groundskeeper, like an employee and not the woman who had borne him a son and taken his name as her own.

For all his cruelty, his impossible expectations, his indifference to her needs, the worst thing of all was how little their marriage meant to him beyond the role she filled and the image she projected by his side.

"I'll have an early supper laid for you, my lord, and we can discuss the issue then. You look exhausted, husband. Did you ride that mule the entire way from London?" She would never stop trying to inject some levity and affection into their relationship, but as usual, Lord Burghley met her attempts with annoyance.

"I am quite well, lady wife. Come, there is no time to sup."

He was not well.

Her husband was eight years her senior but looked older. As Mildred neared thirty, Burghley looked more haggard every time she saw him, and he had not been virile in his youth. His short stature grew more crooked by the day, and his ink-stained hands were like birds' talons; only his graying beard was hale and hearty.

Mildred followed him as he sped through the dark shadows of the manor. The memory of the strange wolf returned to her as they passed a painting of an ancient hunt. When she awoke that morning, she had been determined to tell her husband about her encounter, but now she wasn't sure. It was the sensible thing to do; the creature could be dangerous. But her instincts told her to keep the wolf to herself.

Lady Mildred Cecil might have been a baroness, wed to the Secretary of State, but she was at her core a wild thing, and she would not ignore her instincts.

The world could lace her in tight stays, cover her in pounds of gilded velvet, and tease her hair into jeweled ropes, but it could not take her animal heart.

Lord Burghley's quick stride ate up the carpeted halls, and soon they found themselves within the cramped study her husband used during the brief periods he stayed at Burghley House.

She hated this room. It smelled of sealing wax, parchment, and iron ink — bland but suffocating.

Like her husband.

He took a seat at his desk cluttered and covered with a fine layer of dust because he wouldn't allow her near his personal correspondence.

Mildred thought about sitting, but she knew better than to expect courtesy from her own husband. He wanted her at attention, as if she were one of his clerks, turning in ink-splotched ledgers or losing his letters.

"I've heard ugly rumors about the youngest Tansy child.

Witchcraft on my estate." Her husband spoke in a measured, logical voice. He was a natural-born lawyer.

"Gossip from an alewife, no doubt. Margret Boucher has a vendetta against Mr. Tansy. Must we indulge the whimsy of our tenants?" Mildred affected the weariness in her tone that she felt every day, even as terror coursed through her.

Her heart clenched as she thought of Ness Tansy and her kind eyes spinning her wheel while she sang sweet songs to keep time with the pedal. Mildred couldn't see the gilded matrix of life that threaded her soul to her body like a physick, but she could sense it.

The power that fueled her hothouse and elixirs was the same power that made Ness Tansy's red madder dye true. But Mildred was a mage by birth, and Ness a witch by law, a secret Mildred had kept between herself and the seventeen-year-old for over a year. She had no intention of exposing the girl now.

It seemed all their secrecy had been for nothing, because her husband might know. He'd either suspected it long before Mildred discovered the girl herself, or someone close to Ness had betrayed her.

The average reward for identifying a witch was twenty pounds, which was more than most yeomen farmers and tradesmen made in a year. Mildred would never forgive the men and women who betrayed their own kin to the Witch Finder, but she understood it.

The harvests had been worse than any in memory, and people were going hungry. Not everyone could earn their living through the wool trade, and there were entire households wasting away in the north.

Her husband did not speak right away. Mildred wondered if she could excuse herself from the conversation on some pretense of seeing to Robert or the cook, but then his icy eyes narrowed.

"Ugly rumors may well become hard truths, and I would rather not be caught unawares if witchcraft is so near our home." Elizabeth's Privy Council was pressuring her to strengthen the Witchcraft Codes; they wanted more money for Witch Finders, more public burnings.

Her husband hid his true feelings on the matter, even from her, but she suspected he was among those who were pushing for stricter penalties. How would it look if the Lincolnshire Sheriff and local constabulary discovered his own wife had been harboring a witch in their midst?

Mildred suppressed a shudder and vowed that no one, not her husband, nor his mistress the Queen, would discover Ness's secret.

"You know what is best. I only beg that you tell me how I may help you." She curtsied, pausing with her head low and tilted away from his cold gaze. He let her linger in that uncomfortable position long enough to communicate his general displeasure or his power, then dismissed her.

"Very well, now fetch the ledgers. I am lax in my duties to the estate," She could have reminded him that he had yet to find an error in her accounting, but it would only sour his mood further, and she needed time to warn Ness that Lord Burghley was home, and where he laid his eyes a Witch Finder was soon to follow.

# MILDRED

Three days later and Mildred found her husband's presence even more suffocating than usual.

"My lady, there is a matter with the winter shearing."

Mildred was on her way into the workshop to gather some comfrey when the housekeeper stopped her. Mrs. Thomas was an elderly woman who'd been Mildred's maid before her marriage. She was loyal, discreet, and, above all, observant.

"Lord Burghley's post," Mrs. Thomas whispered when Mildred stepped close to the woman.

She looked down at the stack of letters in Mrs. Thomas's weathered hands. At the top of the pile was a letter with her husband's seal in red wax, addressed to Hugh Boswick in Stamford.

Boswick was the sixth generation in a long line of gentry, and the Witch Finder General for Lincolnshire. It could only mean that her husband was confident enough to bring the man into the investigation.

"If he's writing to Boswick, then he means to send for the man soon. Thank you, Mrs. Thomas." Mildred didn't dare tamper with the letter. Her husband had no skill at magic, but he didn't need to enchant his letters to keep them private. Lord Burghley was a master letter-locker, and she could never re-fold the letter in his special way.

"Yes, my lady." Mrs. Thomas curtsied and turned to go.

Before the woman could get far, Mildred whispered, "I will be retiring early this evening. My stomach pains me. If my husband asks, let him know I have taken ill." Lady Burghley often took to her bed when her husband came calling, and Mrs. Thomas was skilled at keeping the man from her mistress's chamber.

"Very good." The housekeeper shuffled off as quickly as she could toward Lord Burghley's valet.

Mildred sped up her pace. She would need dried briar rose, crushed walnuts, and the stash of coins her father had sent her with when she'd left his house a decade prior. He didn't trust the Cecils, and he'd wanted her to have some money of her own. But her fantasies of running off to the Low Countries be damned; Ness could use that money to try her luck in Ireland or Wales. If she kept her head down and did not use her magic, then no one could accuse her, though she did not envy the poor young woman. If she had been forced to hide her magic, she might have gone insane.

If Mildred hurried, she could slip out to the back garden while her husband remained preoccupied with his ledgers. There was no one in Burghley House who knew the lord's lands like her. She and Ness would make it to Grimsby in time to purchase berth on a trading vessel easily, and Lady Burghley would be back in her bed before midnight.

On her way to enact her hasty plan, Robert intercepted her.

"Mother! I have something wonderful to show you. Come!"

Her melancholy child was so rarely excited that she was

powerless to deny him as he took her hand and led her to the workroom they shared.

"I feel very poorly, love. Let's see, and then I'll have to go to bed early."

He led her to the workroom, where her husband's looming presence overshadowed their comfortable, magical space.

Lord Burghley looked entirely too pleased, which was always a bad omen. He was rarely happy unless it was at the expense of others.

"Ah, good boy, you've found your lady mother. Now, show her your new spell." Lord Burghley clasped his hands in front of his body and smiled, but it was his courtier's smile. There was calculation behind it, and Mildred shuddered to think what that meant, even for his own son.

Before she could stop him, Robert pulled a cloth from a lumpy shape on his workbench. The sight beneath it made Mildred gasp.

Harry, Robert's pet raven, lay dead on the cold wood. Its neck was twisted unnaturally, and its beak hung open in a silent call. It was only three nights ago that she'd brushed gently across the creature's being and spoken to it in the dark sky.

Robert loved that bird. The servants joked that it was his only friend, and sadly, they weren't far off.

Mildred was too stunned and heartbroken to stop what happened next.

Robert's eyes went white as the temperature in the room dropped and curled his breath into smoke. Her son drew power from the ancient bones under Burghley House. The earth beneath them groaned as if something deep and dead was stirring.

Did they know that the builders had covered an old pagan mound to erect her husband's shining house of reason, that the dead were as constant as a house cat under their feet? With dawning horror, she realized that part of Robert knew. He sensed the dead, and the dead called back to him.

This was not a lesson she had taught her son; this was no pruning of an orange tree.

The bird twitched violently as a strangled wheeze escaped its open beak. It curled in on itself and then flattened out as its feathered form shuddered. A sickening, wet, cracking sound echoed through the room as the poor bird's neck snapped back into a natural position.

As sudden as death itself, the raven was now standing upright, staring into her son's face as if waiting for instruction. Robert reached out, and the bird affectionately nuzzled its head against his hand, as if it were still alive and could feel its master's warmth.

But that undead monstrosity was no longer Harry, the friendly, chatty raven that kept her son company. It was an echo of that thing, its soul had departed into the place where birds nest between lives.

This thing was now a dead, twisted approximation of Robert's desires, and it would never be anything more.

"We had to snap the neck again to show you, but Harry is all better now. Better than new, right, Father?" Their son looked up into his father's eyes and smiled.

Lord Burghley's laugh made her blood run cold as he reached over to pat Robert on the head. "Just so. Now take Harry out so that he can get used to his wings again. He needs his exercise after putting on such a good show."

Their son tapped his right shoulder, signaling Harry to take his usual spot, and the bird settled itself as if it were still Robert's living companion. Mildred wondered if her son understood the gravity of his actions, if he knew that his pet was no longer a living, thinking creature. Harry was nothing more than a receptacle for the young boy's ego, a dark mirror that would reflect nothing true.

Robert went to hug his mother, but his face fell when she flinched away from him. Guilt twisted alongside her horror; she didn't want Robert to feel tainted by his power. It was horrific, but that didn't mean he was wrong or broken. Before she could explain herself, he was gone, running down the hallway as his undead familiar croaked like an echo of a true bird.

"Did you know?" Her husband's question cut through her grief and reminded her that both she and Robert now stood on perilous ground with Lord Burghley. She had given him a son, but she did not know if he would strike them both down now that he knew the fruit of their union was a necromancer.

Necromancy was the only magical arte forbidden to the nobility. Mildred's own grandfather had been buried alive for heinous crimes committed in the name of his diabolic magic.

The power had skipped two generations, and her family had learned to suppress the rumor of their fallen patriarch, but perhaps her husband was furious that the wife he'd taken for access to her magical lineage harbored such a dark gift?

"I did not suspect it, but I now know there were some signs. We had the culling lesson yesterday, and he seemed too keen. I should have known."

Lord Burghley did not hold women in high esteem, perhaps because he was ruled so harshly by his mistress the Queen. Mildred often used his prejudice to her advantage.

It was easy to play dumb when her husband assumed she was a simpleton.

Lord Burghley's snake-like gaze held her like a vise, but he said nothing for long moments. She couldn't take the uncertainty any longer and cracked under the weight of his eyes.

"Please don't hurt him."

For the first time in a decade, her husband's thick eyebrows rose, and confusion colored the creases of his brow. "Hurt him? Are you mad, woman?"

Relief coursed through her breast so fast that she felt momentarily dizzy. "Thank God, thank God," she muttered.

If the lord was upset by her outburst, he didn't dwell on it.

"Robert is my son, my legacy. He will serve our Queen when I am gone, and his powers will be a boon to the Crown. We may even learn to wield them against the tide of vampires devouring the continent. They will soon turn their fangs on England, mark my words."

"You would sacrifice our son's soul for England? His magic will devour him. No good can come from calling out to the dead."

Her husband was the insane one.

Fury broke across Lord Burghley's face like a summer storm. He looked as though he wanted to strike her, but that was one line he had never crossed in their marriage. Not for lack of desire, but she suspected he did not want to sully himself with something so base as beating his wife.

"Superstitious nonsense. You sound like a blighted papist, terrified of old bones and feeble spirits. We are modern men now; the light of reason will shine upon the powers Robert possesses and allow him to wield them as a useful tool."

Mildred fell to her knees and gripped the hem of his sable cloak; she knew better than to appeal to his sense of mercy, but she was overcome with agony. She had to protect her son from his scheming father.

"Please, you must not encourage this power. I will send for my father. He will come and tell you about our family. Of the horror this magic has wrought on the Cooke line. I beg you, please."

He shoved her off him, and she fell back against the legs of the sturdy workbench, her beautiful crimson cloth-of-gold petticoat, soiled with dust as she wallowed in the dirt beneath Lord Burghley.

"I do not need a lecture from your father. The matter is settled. Robert will accompany me to London when this witchcraft business is concluded; be sure to say your good-byes in that time, madam."

He left her then, in a heap, sobbing as night fell on the estate. She allowed herself an hour to wallow in her wretchedness. Mildred knew she would lose her son, but she had not thought it would happen so fast and so brutally.

The thought of watching his light dim with each passing year as the foulness of his magic overtook her sweet son's heart was a fresh agony she wasn't sure she could bear.

But she had to bear it; because Ness needed her, and perhaps if she could thwart her husband's attempt at pulling a witch up onto the stake in Lincolnshire she could buy some time for Robert.

It was a mad, hopeless endeavor, but Mildred had to move forward and try to save those dear to her.

# SYMON

Symon left his companion in Grimbsy to investigate the witchcraft rumors swilling around the little shanty village. They overheard whispers that the lord was harboring a witch among his tenants, which meant one of the rare-bloods they sought would soon be accused.

The vampires did not know why, but their mates were usually mages or carried the power latent within them. The law of Christian Europe and the Isles branded common magic witchcraft, which meant vampires were often hunting on the heels of Witch Finders.

It was perilous for all involved but had a bonus of making the vampires' offer of asylum irresistible to most.

As Symon sped through the lord's wood of Lincolnshire, he thought of the earth elemest, Lady Burghley. She would not go willingly, not with her status and position. He did not relish snatching an unwilling mortal from her bed and hoped that he would find her running through the brush in her human skin. There was something strange about the lady.

Many noblewomen possessed magic, but not many made themselves prey under the cover of night.

Perhaps he could seduce her into the boat. The thought of pulling her screaming from the woods made his stomach flip. For all of his sins, forcing his will on another was not among them. But he could give her a heart-pounding chase and a mutually pleasurable capture for both of them if she was keen.

By the gods of Night and Shadow, he should not think of a rare-blood in such ways. Jaded as he was, he maintained decorum around their Precious Ones. No vampire wanted their future mate to give themselves to another, and he didn't need to give Centurion Yasha Darkov another reason to deliver a sun-lashing.

He bounded over fallen logs and sprinted through the thick underbrush with ease. In the half-moon dark of the forest, he could inhabit his truest wolf form: a dire beast the size of a draft horse. The bounding steps of his massive paws made the trees shake and the small, furred denizens of the forest dig deep into their burrows.

He had not gone far when the scent of heaven hit his sensitive nose like hellfire.

Strawberries assaulted him.

He had not thought of food in centuries and found the pottage and stale bread mortals consumed nauseating, but something about the scent made the beast inside him riot. Red, delectable berries, ripened by the sun and hot on his tongue, teased at his mind as he followed his nose to the source.

Last night, the delicate aroma of overripe strawberry had lingered like a forgotten perfume against the body of Lady Burghley's rabbit, but now it was all-consuming. It lit up ancient urges within him and quickened his pace toward the origin of the scent.

There was another scent wafting around that sweet aroma; pleasant, but not *his*.

The raw, acrid stink of fear twisted around both distinct flavors, and his keen ears picked up the sounds of heavy skirts dragging through the mud and hearts pounding in the darkness.

He must have been half a mile away from the two mortals, but the closer he got, the clearer they became; two women running from the stink of iron and smoked meat.

Soldiers. They were being pursued by soldiers.

It was never a good thing to be chased by careless men in armor, in any country or century.

Symon pumped his wolf form through with his tainted blood, drawing on the power of his clan to move swifter than a common wolf could dream of.

When he burst through a dense, thorny rosebush and landed in front of the two women. They let out a shriek, alerting the soldiers at their heels to their presence. Heavy boots crashed through the forest, cracking twigs and scattering fallen leaves, but he remained frozen.

A goddess stared down at him.

With a shaking, sweet voice that would follow him into his long years and down into the underworld, she uttered, "You will come no closer, wolf."

As if her words alone could drive him away.

Nothing would separate them now, not an army of blood bags in armor, or an ocean, or the sun itself.

Her hair was as red as an open vein, and her eyes green like loamy moorland. She was a soft thing, with a lush body hidden beneath suffocating layers of velvet. Her slender nose and oval-shaped face gave her a delicate grace, even with the surprise and terror in her eyes.

That mouth should do nothing but smile while he fed her delicacies from the Levant. She should not be running from anything, because nothing could be more terrifying than him or what he would do to anyone who dared harm what was his.

He would have rather stayed there, his paws rooted into the soft earth, and counted the dusting of fine freckles across her cheeks, but their pursuers had found them.

There was no thought; what followed was instinct alone.

The clandestine campaigns that led Terra Noxa into hostile countries were meant to be completed with absolute stealth. Slip in and slip out. No meddling with local politics or picking fights with soldiers. But he didn't intend to leave any man standing long enough to go telling tall tales.

There were four men, brutish and stinking. He pounced on the first soldier, landing hard enough to slam the mortal into the ground. The impact probably killed the bastard instantly, but Symon was in a rage and snapped his jaws across the soldier's face before ripping his head away with half the soldier's skull in his maw.

The other brave souls dropped their pikes and turned to flee, but they didn't get far. Their cheap breastplates failed to cover their vulnerable backs, and Symon ripped out the spine of one, then slashed his claws across the other two.

They bled out in seconds, soaking the earth in their filthy life. In any other circumstance, he might have taken the opportunity to gorge himself on their blood, but it smelled rotten compared to the fine, ripe strawberry behind him.

Symon caught up with the women in a few bounds and cornered them against the drooping arms of a great oak. The fear stench made his stomach curdle. He didn't want his strawberry to fear him; he had destroyed her enemies. She should rejoice and give him head scratches.

Symon crouched low until he was crawling on his belly toward the two women as they clung to one another, whimpering and flattening his ears back so that they knew he meant them no harm, though the message was somewhat ruined by the bloody gore caked over his snout.

"What's it doing?" the other woman asked, and his red-haired goddess moved her body to protect her companion.

"I don't think he wants to hurt us," she whispered; and inched closer to him.

Symon's tail thumped against the ground in a desperate staccato that made the ground around him shake. His strawberry stepped between his massive paws that plowed into the wet earth. Even seated, her shoulders came up to his snout, and floppy ears dwarfed her small hands as she reached up and ran her fingers through the silken fur that coated his forehead.

"I met you last night, didn't I? How did you get so much bigger?" Her voice was low and soothing. Between her sweet words and the gentle touch against his head, Symon sank against her and nuzzled the fiery-haired, sweet-smelling woman.

Her clear, bright laughter filled the woods as she teetered and wobbled against his weight when his head bumped into her chest.

"Careful, madam, you show that beast any more affection, and you'll find yourself with a new lapdog. He's terribly disobedient." Stefan Orrens stepped from the shadows, and Symon felt his soft little strawberry stiffen against him.

His rumbling growl stopped Stefan in his tracks as Symon's paws closed around the woman, who was now the most precious being in the world to him.

Pity that he didn't have a way of communicating that to her.

"Forgive me, I am being unconscionably rude." Stefan bowed to the women and removed his cap. "I am Ambassador Orrens, representative of Terra Noxa and the Council of Night. And you must be Ness Tansy." He turned to the girl, who had almost completely slipped from Symon's attention.

Stefan had done his due diligence in the village, at least, and he no doubt scented that they now had two women to smuggle out of England.

The girl, Ness, was their original target. She was still crouched down on the ground, wearing a stained red kirtle and a plain white veil that concealed the color of her hair. She must have been ten years younger than Lady Burghley, no more than a teenager.

"That is correct, sir." The girl stood and gave Stefan a brief curtsy. "My mistress and I were running from the estate."

"Mistress. I see. Lady Burghley, I assume?"

Symon tilted his head as his wolf eyes surveyed the woman. He began to regain some of his human mind from his wild shape, and he slowly realized how much finer her dress was than Ness's.

This noble-born woman had risked much to save the young girl from the Witch Finders. Highborn or not, aiding an accused witch could be a death sentence.

She was delightfully odd. His mate was noble, and yet she ran through the woods like a pagan wise woman in the skin of a rabbit and aided young witches in the dead of night. He could not have wished for a more intriguing lover.

"You are correct, but what are you doing here? England is no safer for your kind," Lady Burghley said.

Symon nuzzled against her shoulder and then stood up.

He did not want her to see the hard, messy pain of his transformation, but they had little time, and there was much to discuss before the Witch Finder stalked the woods himself when his men did not return.

Before Stefan could answer her question, the sound of Symon's snapping bones and tearing muscle filled the small clearing. Lady Burghley stumbled away from him as the mass of his wolf's body folded in on itself and back into the form of a man.

He wasn't ashamed of his nudity; quite the contrary, he reveled in the way his mate raked her gaze down the long, lean lines of his well-earned musculature. She didn't flinch or look away when her eyes landed on his throbbing cock, either, which sent an inconvenient jolt of need up his spine as he stiffened further.

Did she notice the shock of white hair above his right eye? The silver stripe among his thick dark hair and his defined jawline had attracted his sire to him centuries before. Symon wanted her to see and admire him in a way he'd not desired in his second life. He did spare a moment to consider Amaranth, but he couldn't muster the guilt or the longing from before.

There would only be his ripe, pretty little strawberry from now until the end of his nights.

"Good gods, man! Cover yourself in the presence of ladies." A bundle of clothing smacked into his chest, hurled at him by Stefan, who stepped between him and the women present while he hurriedly dressed.

"I don't think I offended you, did I, strawberry?" he asked Lady Burghley, but she didn't answer him.

The flush of her cheeks was gratifying as she looked away, though.

They weren't supposed to use their inhuman speed or strength in front of their Precious Ones. It tended to upset them, but Symon had already displayed his shift to the mortals. It was a little late for manners.

After a few heartbeats, Symon stood before the women in his black leathers and boots. Only his red eyes and pointed eyeteeth betrayed his true nature.

"Now, let's start over in a more civilized manner." Stefan's face grew serious as he stepped towards young Ness. "Miss Tansy, I am here to deliver you to sanctuary within Terra Noxa. No harm shall come to you, on my word."

Lady Burghley was sharp. She understood what his companion was saying right away.

"You didn't ask her if she wanted to go. You intend to take her."

Stefan was a gentle soul, despite his nature. The apologetic look on his face was sincere.

"It is my duty to deliver you from your persecution. I will not allow the Witch Finders to take you, Miss Tansy, but I cannot give you a choice in the matter. I will, however, never lie to you."

"I'm going with him," the young woman blurted out, and Symon sighed in relief.

He was afraid that he'd have to fight them both to get the women to safety.

Lady Burghley spun around toward her young friend, "You aren't safe with them. We can buy you passage on the next ship out. You could go to Wales or Ireland like we planned."

Ness was young, but Symon could tell she was a clever girl. She could see the reality of her situation.

"I'd still be in reach of the Witch Finders and under the Witchcraft Codes. Ireland won't be safe forever if your husband gets his way. My best chance is on the continent. I won't need to hide there."

Lady Burghley shook her head so violently that curled locks of her red hair escaped the pearl-studded plait looped over her forehead.

"You can't make such an impulsive decision."

The girl had already made up her mind. She touched Lady Burghley's shoulder and smiled.

"You are a force to be reckoned with, Mildred, but even

you can't stop these men from taking me. I'll be all right. Wolves and vampires are better company than constables and Witch Finders."

Symon couldn't help but grin; he liked the girl's spirit. She would make a fine mate to one of his kin in the coming years, and until then, they would protect and educate her.

"It's settled then." His voice felt raw and disused, as it always did after a transformation. "Say your goodbyes. Stefan will escort Ness to the boat, while I make sure Lady Burghley makes it home without running afoul of more witch hunters."

A look that could scorch wood appeared on Stefan's face, but nothing could be done about it.

Mildred Burghley was now Symon's responsibility alone.

# MILDRED

There was a tense moment between the two vampires that felt like the prelude to violence. Stefan, with his blue eyes and deceptively human smile, spoke in a sharp, clipped tongue she didn't recognize. It was lyrical even as it spilled out in angry bursts from his mouth.

The vampire by her side, who had yet to introduce himself, spoke three strange words, which ended their argument on a cold, sharp note.

She hated not knowing what they were saying, but there was no time pry into their private quarrel. Despite her husband's despotic nature, he was not wrong about everything; humans had good reason to be wary of vampires, even more so when they risked sneaking into a hostile country to aid a peasant they knew virtually nothing about.

They were creatures of darkness, not curiosity. So why could she not stop staring at the wolfish vampire by her side?

She knew they were strong and possessed dark magic that could bewitch or eviscerate a mortal, but she'd had no idea that they could change their form.

It fascinated her, along with the wolfish vampire's handsome face, what little of it she could see in the dark. Beyond the pleasing, hard angles of his square face and the severe, thick eyebrows over ember red eyes, one feature stood out.

The shock of white hair on the right side of his brow. It was strange and incongruent, but Mildred found the contrast precious.

The imperfection made his beauty touchable.

Mildred gripped her hands tight by her sides to keep herself from reaching up and running her hands through the silken silver.

None of this was about her or her disturbing attraction to the vampire who had chased her in the body of a wolf the night before. Time was precious, and she couldn't waste her last moments with one of her dearest friends staring at the beautiful, dark man by her side.

Ness had made her decision, and though Mildred disagreed, she would not cheapen the girl's attempt at agency after being denied it for so long.

"I can't read or write yet, but once I learn how, I'll smuggle letters to you, I promise, miss." Ness was sweet, and despite the precariousness of her journey ahead with the vampires, Mildred couldn't help but smile as they embraced.

The thought of going back to her lonely existence, punctuated only by the bright spot of her son and the cold gloom of her husband, was crushing.

Now that the excitement had died down, the reality of all that she was about to lose solidified. Robert and Ness, possibly within days of one another now that her husband wouldn't have a witch to persecute.

At least she had succeeded in spiriting Ness away from the Witch Finders; no matter what happened next, Mildred could be proud of that.

Stefan gave Mildred another bow. "Thank you, Lady

Burghley. You are far more brave and decent than your countrymen."

She couldn't help but agree with the fresh-faced vampire; her kin and countrymen were almost irredeemable.

"And you are not so bloodthirsty as the Queen's curmudgeonly ministers say. Safe travels, Mr. Orrens."

Stefan gave her a soft smile and flashed a pointed look at Symon before offering his arm to Ness.

Ness and Stefan hurried away, disappearing into the dark wood, leaving her alone with the handsome, imposing vampire. The back of her neck prickled with the weight of his eyes before she turned around to face him.

Why did it feel so delicious to be pinned down by his red gaze?

"You, sir, are unforgivably rude. You killed four men for me this evening, and I don't know your name." It was un-lady like to jest about the death of four guards, but they'd been doing the bidding of the Witch Finder, so she could spare them very little pity.

The mysterious vampire bowed low, his red gaze traveling up the length of her body as he righted himself. Then he took her hand, and rather than brushing his lips across her knuckles, he turned her wrist up and placed a warm kiss against her pounding pulse point.

His mouth was too close to her delicate blue veins for comfort, and yet it wasn't fear that quickened her heart. Mildred had been married for over a decade and had never felt such a powerful desire communicated in so simple a touch.

"Symon de Vitre, at your service, my lady." His voice was low and rumbling, like the deep growl of his wolf. The sound of it was pleasant, with the echo of the wilderness in his words, as if he spent years without speaking as a human.

Mildred found the untamed quality of his lips, his voice, his bold eyes intoxicating.

She stepped away from him and set off toward the estate. They would need to take the long way around through the orchard and the back gardens so that the Witch Finder wouldn't lose any more men, not that she wanted more soldiers terrorizing the peasantry. She'd rather not deepen the investigation while Ness was not yet on a boat bound for the continent.

The vampire, Symon, kept an easy pace beside her, and his heavy gaze never left her. He navigated beside her in the near dark as if she were a guiding willow light.

"You are the Baroness Burghley, I take it? Do you have a Christian name, or did you give that up for your title?" he asked as they made their way carefully through the slim portal on a thorn-covered thicket that encircled the orchard.

"I have given up much for this title, but never that. My name is Mildred."

Most women of her station would tack their pride onto their husband's name, but she never felt worthy of it. The success of their house had so little to do with her. Even the most callous of political marriages became calculated partnerships in time. But not so with her husband; William did not think her his equal in any regard.

She gave the vampire her Christian name, the name she thought of as belonging only to her. Perhaps she should have been more cautious with it, but something about the wildness of him made her want to test fate and caution.

"It is strange that you would assist a common girl. I understand that not even your noble titles can protect you from the Witch Finder's pyre," he said, as she stumbled over an unseen log.

His warm, steady hands gripped her elbow before she could trip over her skirts into a patch of sharp thorns.

It was true. She risked more than her reputation in sparing Ness from the pyre, but she was insulted by the surprise in Symon's voice.

"There is nothing more noble than breaking unjust laws," she said curtly, and then promptly changed the subject. She shouldn't care what he thought of her, but she didn't want to dissect her motives with the vampire by her side.

"You don't sound like a Frenchman," she said after a few beats.

His surname, de Vitre, was uniquely Franco-sounding.

He laughed, quirking up his full, expressive lips in a grin. "I've spent so much time in Wallachia and Italy that I fear my mother tongue has softened."

Mildred tried to imagine what it would be like to live long enough to forget the place where she had been born and educated. It should have been a horrifying thought, but she found it strangely comforting, as if there was some distant hope that she, too, could leave behind her constrictive, narrow, little life.

It was a privileged existence, but paid for with her peace.

"Where did you come from?"

He looked away from her, and Mildred realized that her question was a little too pointed.

The vampires were carving up Charles V's Holy Roman Empire while he lay on his sickbed, and the last news from the continent was that they'd taken a swath of land from Milan to Flanders. He could have come from any of those conquered places.

"You don't need to answer that, though I'm unlikely to tell my husband. The Secretary of State would sooner take council from a stablehand than his wife." It was dangerous to speak ill of her husband, even to the servants, and a guilty thrill surged through her as she loosened her tongue in front of the vampire.

"Then he is a fool." The vampire's hot breath curled at her bare neck, sending a pleasant shiver into her belly. "You have mettle and courage, the likes of which your feckless husband could not dream."

Mildred should push him away and insist on propriety while they were alone, but the half-moon chose that moment to shine from behind the cover of cloud and bathe his face in silver.

His large, expressive eyes and generous mouth softened the severity of his square jaw. Symon was almost a foot taller than her, but he didn't loom; even with his breath caressing her bare neck, she sensed an air of reverence about the way he looked at her.

She wanted to touch him.

Naming the desire, even in her own mind, was terrifying, but she couldn't deny it. When she met his eyes, silence stretched between them as his gaze lingered on her lips.

Perhaps he could smell her need and neglect in the air. If he could take the form of a wolf, then it stood to reason that he could sniff out the curling heat at her core, or the way her nipples hardened to painful buds under her dress and shift.

Who would know if she stole a kiss from a vampire? She had already broken the law; why not bend her marriage vows, too?

Her mother had always said she was too much in love with the rutting, eating, wild things of the earth, that her magic was too free, and that it would lead her astray if she did not tamp down her animal passions.

Perhaps her mother had been right, but she had died an unhappy, unloved woman bringing Mildred's youngest brother into the world. Mildred would rather live astray than die unfulfilled and good.

"I see the orchard ahead." Her courage failed her, and she pulled away from Symon.

A companionable silence fell between them as they slipped through the neat and ordered apple trees and into the manicured garden. The dark outline of her hothouse and the soft fairy lights of the willow lanterns she'd left on earlier were a welcome sight.

Mildred didn't want to end her adventure so soon, but she dared not linger outside much longer. Her husband would no doubt be awake, waiting on news from the Witch Finder and his men's pursuit. They didn't know she was involved and probably never would. Mildred had gotten Ness up and out of bed well before the soldiers had stormed the Tansy household. The poor girl hadn't a chance to say goodbye to her parents, but at least they'd had a head start in the woods.

Mildred led Symon into a dark shadow on the east wall of the manor, near the back entrance into the kitchens. The dark casement windows assured her that the cook was well abed, and she would be able to access the servants' stairs without any of the belowstairs staff noticing her. In the darkness, her fine dress was the same as any servant's gown.

Before she could say her goodbyes, the wolfish vampire wrapped one of his arms around her waist and pulled her into the dark lee of the house. Cold, wet stone pressed against her back and chilled the skin of Mildred's neck where her partlet would have covered if she had not lost it in the chase.

"I must protest," Mildred whispered, but her breathlessness revealed the lie in her resistance.

The vampire's red eyes caught the moon-glow and reflected it back like rubies as he covered her with his broad, warm body.

"You must, but you don't mean it, lady." His rough whisper fluttered across her lips as they shared breath.

"Step aside, or I will wake the house," she hissed.

Symon de Vitre grinned. The long, elegant points of his eyeteeth flashed in the night. They should have terrified her, but she found herself captivated by his feral grin. She couldn't help but wonder what they might feel like pressed against her lips, or running down her neck.

"I won't stop you." His rough whisper curled into the night as one of his big, heated palms ran up her side. His touch stoked a fire in her that she had thought long dead.

"You have not had a man in years." He leaned forward and inhaled the overheated air between them. The brush of his nose from her neck to her jaw forced a shiver from her body. "Your husband is twice the fool. How could he keep his hands off such perfect skin?"

Her body jolted as he planted sharp kisses back down her neck. To her shame, she arched up against him, baring herself to the wild, shadow-touched man.

A vampire bite was supposed to be pain and horror. They latched onto the neck of their victim and bit down on their windpipe, drinking long enough to drain their prey before ripping out the poor mortal's throat.

Or so she'd read, by sources who'd claimed to witness vampire attacks firsthand.

But there was no violence in his kiss. The hunger of his mouth and his touches were pure and carnal.

God forgive her, she loved it.

She gasped into the night as his kiss on her neck deepened, the prick of his fangs denting her unbroken flesh forced quick, desperate little breaths from her slack lips.

"Are you going to devour me?" Her voice sounded so strange, as if his wildness was catching.

"Yes, but I plan to take my time, sweet little strawberry."

His lips crashed into her mouth, and his tongue curled past her teeth. It was a bruising, wet kiss that took her sanity along with her breath. Mildred moaned into it, her hands clawing at his shoulders as he pressed her into the icy wall of the manor.

A deep, rumbling growl tickled down her throat, and he pulled himself away with a desperate gasp. The vampire stumbled away from her, wiping at his mouth and pinning her in place with those ruby-tinted eyes.

"Tomorrow night," he whispered, desperate madness in his wide eyes and snarling teeth. "Meet me in the orchard at midnight, and I will show you the pleasure of a true hunter's chase." He sounded strangled and clumsy, as if too aroused to string proper English together.

That made two of them.

"I would be a fool to give myself to a vampire," she whispered into the night, more for her benefit than his.

"And you will regret it for the rest of your life if you do not," he answered her, and then bowed.

He turned and then paused, speaking over his shoulder. "I won't hurt you. This I swear, but know that you are my prey, and I do not release my quarry until it is mine."

Then he was gone, melting into the shadows. Mildred stood there, pressed against the manor, straining to listen for evidence that he'd ever been there.

She was beginning to convince herself that the entire encounter was the result of her touch-starved heart when a chilling howl pierced the night.

# MILDRED

She ran a hand over her neck, checking for blood, but found none. His fangs had teased her flesh but not cut into it. There was no pain, only the phantom, toe-curling caress of that vicious mouth.

Mildred might have stayed like that all night if not for the danger that pressed in on her. Any moment now, the Witch Finder would discover his men butchered in the forest, and they would no doubt come to Burghley House and report to her husband directly.

If she meant to live through the night, then she had to make her way into her chambers, where Mrs. Thomas was waiting to get her to bed. There was no reason to suspect that her husband may enter her rooms, but it wasn't something she would put past him.

It was best to err towards caution where her husband was concerned. Lord Burghley thought little of her intellect, and she didn't want to give him a reason to believe otherwise.

The hearth was banked down to cherry-red embers as she stole through the dark room, making her way by memory in the darkness. When she got to the servant stairs at the back of the room, she drew a quick firefly sigil in the air and summoned three soft, glowing lights that hovered around her like miniature willow lanterns.

There were no true fireflies in England, but her magic allowed her to borrow the light from insects a continent away. The lights were weak but sufficient that she could navigate the narrow steps and ascend to the upper floor of the manor. The only servant that ought to be awake at this hour was Mrs. Thomas, but Mildred crept along like a thief, with an abundance of caution.

She was nearly in the hallway in the south wing that would lead into her bedroom when a clear, silver bell chimed in her mind. The spell she'd woven into her husband's study was discreet and effective. An artificer had enchanted the obsidian inlay in the room's doorway to prevent scrying spells, but her husband was no mage, so it had been easy to add a simple proximity bell over it.

Mildred did not like being surprised by her husband and had laid similar spells through the house tuned to Lord Cecil's life signature. The pleasant little ring could only be heard by her, and it had saved her more trouble than she could count.

Mildred broke the sigil keeping her fireflies near, and they dissipated like dewdrops. She crept into the darkness and crouched down to peer into the office through the tiny sliver of gold in the doorway. The old stone of the house knew her and cradled her body in silence at her request. The house darkened over her body as she settled down to watch what terrible plans her husband was making with the other man in the room.

It was the Witch Finder, Boswick.

He lounged in a high-backed chair near the fireplace as Lord Burghley loomed above him, leaning into the carved relief of the Burghley coat of arms with their house motto in scrolling Latin beneath it.

*Cor unum via una*. One heart, one way.

If the Witch Finder General understood the darkness at the core of Burghley's motto, he wouldn't be lounging so freely in front of her husband. Her view framed the two men as if they were sitting in a portrait. The deadly calm in Lord Burghley's eyes reflected the gilded fire, but she knew him well. Tension bound his shoulders, and his fist, resting on the mantle, was balled into a tight grip.

"Are you certain the girl had an accomplice?" Lord Burghley asked, his eyes downcast into the fire.

"She must have. There's no other explanation. No slop-headed peasant girl could dispatch four grown men so efficiently. I believe there are vampires in our midst. It is fascinating, you know, how they always pop up when we start cracking down on witches. They must be in league." The Witch Finder was a spindly man, with limbs too long and a thin, un-serious mouth that did not seem capable of holding a secret if his life depended on it.

"I will not have such devilry attached to my name." Her husband's words were as sharp and quick as a dagger, but the fool of a Witch Finder didn't realize it was unsheathed for him.

"Fear not, my lord." The Witch Finder stood, his cocky expression narrowing as if he were the predator in the room. "I will ensure your good name remains immaculate, so long as I write my report properly and fail to mention how easily your tenant escaped. Though I sometimes forget the details. A small token of your generosity will ensure my memory works in your favor."

The gall of the man! He was extorting Lord Burghley, the Secretary of State, Her Majesty's closest confidant and head of her Privy Council. Was he an idiot, or terminally ambitious?

"Tedious, but I suppose if needs must. Drink with me, Master Boswick." Lord Burghley never served his own wine, not for friends, nor family. And yet he turned toward his locked wine cabinet, which sat open.

A cold dread skittered through Mildred's belly, and she focused her power into her eyes and nose, calling out into the room with invisible tendrils of knowing.

He couldn't mean to do what she suspected. Could he?

Hugh Bowsick, the Witch Finder General, was oblivious to the motion of Lord Burghley's hands as he worked to uncork and pour the wine. He was chattering on about the wonderful carpets he'd had brought in from Persia and complimenting the size of the lord's estate.

But Mildred shrank back when her magical senses brushed against the bitter taste of hellebore. She knew the plant well. It was used to purge sickness and toxins from the liver after long illnesses. Mildred grew it in her garden, but her home-brewed tinctures were mild compared to the potent magic of the poison Lord Burghley slipped into the Witch Finder's cup.

It must have been hell-crystal, the concentrated form that was used by courtiers and counselors to poison annoying rivals in Elizabeth's court.

Mildred had a choice. She could interrupt the proceedings and reveal herself, or let the Witch Finder drink deep of the poisoned wine.

She had no love for the Witch Finder General, or his kind, but did he deserve to die?

She did the cold math in a heartbeat and remained where she was. Hugh Boswick drained the cup of her husband's fine port wine and did not know he was already dead.

Simple poisons struck the victim immediately, but there

was magic woven into the hellebore crystals her husband used. The effects would not strike the unwitting Witch Finder until later that evening. Some poor servant or the man's long-suffering wife would find him tomorrow morning, dead as though nature had taken him.

It was diabolically brilliant. The man would be long gone from the manor and dead without implicating the lord, not that an accusation of that nature would stand.

Mildred crept back slowly from the door as the men discussed the particulars of the Witch Finder's payment. She moved through the darkened brick halls by touch and tried not to think about the easy way her husband had lied to Boswick, how his face betrayed nothing but disinterest and the barest hint of disdain.

Mrs. Thomas was sitting in the dark when Mildred stumbled out of the hidden servants' door next to her wardrobe. Mrs. Thomas had drawn the curtains to let in some of the half-moon light, but it wasn't enough.

The two women met wordlessly, navigating in the dark by familiarity, not sight. Her dress was filthy and ruined, but she owned dozens more. A fortune in silk, wool, and scarlet cloth of gold lay in her trunks and wardrobes, but she had chosen none of it for herself. She dressed for her noble title and her husband's position as chief courtier, not her own whim. The loss of one of those fine, frivolous gowns felt like a strange victory.

After a few heart-pounding minutes, Mildred had dressed down into her shift. She dismissed Mrs. Thomas with a gentle squeeze of the older woman's shoulder, and she disappeared with her mistress's dress in hand.

There was no time to wash properly, but she splashed some water across her face and hands from the basin near the bed and then crawled under the covers. No sooner had she curled into her pillow and drawn herself up into a tight ball than footsteps sounded down the hall.

They were heavy but careful, and not long after they sounded the handle of her chamber door turned. It was like the crack of a whip in the silence of her dark room. Mildred closed her eyes tight and drew up the steady thrum of the earth beneath Burghley House. She reached into the invisible, gilded green line of magic that snaked through England with invisible lines of magic, and grasped it.

The earth wrapped her in steady, unshakable calm. The sensation rolled over her sleeping body, so that she did not twitch or shudder as the sound of footsteps neared her bed.

Silence stretched on as the magic wrapped around her heart, stilling its terrified beat. There was only one person who would stalk into her room to make sure his wife was where she should be.

Lord Burghley found her bed distasteful, but he sometimes made sure she occupied it at a reasonable hour. It would be unseemly to have a wife who gathered rue by the light of the full moon, or who spent nights in fox burrows chattering with kits into the morning.

It was a habit he'd broken her of viciously in the first year of their marriage.

Mildred longed for her girlhood of running wild into the tangled mists of the night, and she wondered if a new temptation would have her risk her husband's ire.

With eyes sealed shut and her husband looming in the darkness, she thought of Symon's lips. The warm heat and sharpness of his fangs as he kissed her mouth would haunt her all her life.

She wanted more, and as the menacing figure retreated from her room and shut the door, she vowed that she would taste those forbidden lips again.

# SYMON

Symon returned from his stolen moment with Mildred — he'd never call her Lady Burghley again — to their temporary base with Stefan waiting for him.

"Mongrel."

Symon did not know Stefan Orrens well. He could hardly call Stefan a colleague, but Stefan's rage surprised him. Stefan's reputation was that of an even-tempered and uncommonly good-natured vampire.

Symon knew what the Glasul thought of him. He was no more than an animal, a slave to his base desires, and while Stefan wasn't wrong, he had no right to prevent him from claiming his mate.

"Careful, you'll wake our guest, and she's seen enough blood for one evening." Symon stepped away from his companion to root through his saddlebags. He needed to write his Notice of Seclusion as soon as possible. He was not well liked in the cohort, but no one would deny him leave now that he'd found his mate.

"Gods damn you, where is your mate? I've sent word to Flanders, and a boat will be ready for us at dusk. We can't tarry here with the Witch Finders sniffing around," Stefan hissed.

It was striking how little patience Stefan proved to posses when it came to their Precious Ones. Symon wondered how much of that good nature was performance for the sake of mortal mates and how much was genuine feeling.

Symon didn't spare the other vampire a glance as he settled down next to an empty crate and pulled out his ink, quill, and parchment. He lacked practice, but tradition could not be ignored if he was to smuggle the wife of one of the most powerful men in England out of the country.

"She is in her bed, safe at Burghley House. I will not abscond with my mate like a thief in the night." He paused, his red eyes flashing as he considered Stefan. "I need three nights to convince her to follow me willingly."

He did not relish begging, but for Mildred, he'd do what needed to be done.

"Please." He stared down his companion, and they stood at an impasse for what felt like hours. Finally Stefan relented.

"It is within your right of courtship, but I cannot give you the customary time. I am sorry, but I must report the discovery to Centurion Darkov."

Leniency wasn't in Darkov's nature, but Symon's commanding officer could do little about it from Flanders.

"I don't need the traditional time. Her husband is an oaf." Stefan settled down in a chair opposite him and stared down at the old curl of parchment laid out between them on their makeshift table.

"You think she will come so easily? Lady Burghley has a son. No mother would abandon her child so readily."

Symon's hands stilled over the quill as his mind caught up with his companion's words.

That complicated matters a great deal. "What would you prefer me do, take her against her will?"

He didn't have to ask. For all of Stefan's romantic ideals, he was perfectly willing to remove the burden of choice from a rare-blood if it meant they were safe.

"I do not know her yet, but I do know she will not forgive such a thing. I believe she has had too many choices taken from her to stand for such an affront." Symon tried his best to avoid mortals, considering how often they led him into temptation, but he knew what mortal marriages were to the nobility.

Mildred was nothing more than the guarantee of a contract between two patriarchs, her body and her future used to secure the legacy of men who barely figured her into the equation. Mildred's son was not her own; as much as her life was not her own in Burghley House.

He would show her a different way, and she would make the choice to be with him.

But he wasn't above lying to her at first.

"I trust you know what you're doing," Stefan said, and then silence fell between them.

"You shouldn't, because my hands are shaking so badly that I'm not sure I'll be able to finish this letter by dawn," Symon laughed. "Though the thought of the sour-face I'm going to put on Centurion Darkov is adequate inspiration."

Stefan sighed and cast his blue gaze at the sleeping teenager on the far side of the room. At some point he had procured a clean pallet for her to rest on. Symon could tell by her even breath and steady heartbeat that she was deep in sleep.

"Yasha went easy on you. He could have had you killed or lashed. Instead, he gave you a chance to redeem yourself." Stefan was an honorable vampire; he had to be. As a quaestari he was responsible for identifying and protecting their Precious Ones. But he was too idealistic and gave Symon more credit than he deserved.

"Then he is a fool. I could not have found her in worst circumstances. We have three nights to complete courtship that our kin spend months pursuing."

Stefan cast his eyes down toward his own slender hands. He looked like an idealistic student or a monk who had been carried away from a monastery by Danes, but his eyes were old. In the pale candlelight of their dark little lair, Symon saw a glimpse of his companion's true age.

"I have seen long courtships end in tragedy. You are not doomed yet."

Symon could only imagine what horrors Symon had witnessed in his role. Their elders might have the civilized Glasul and the battle addled Balaur fooled, but Symon had a wolf's heart.

He didn't believe in fairytale love stories.

"I bet you have, and yet here we are. Gathering more pretty virgins for our brothers and sisters."

Stefan glared at him sharply.

"Most find happiness; it is not anything like a human marriage."

Symon laughed, "No, death rarely intervenes to shorten the union."

It was a tired argument he'd had with many of his kind as they ransacked Europe and tore apart its monarchies. The human kingdoms of Christendom condemned their common mages as witches and burned them. How convenient that Terra Noxa waited with open arms and safety.

Stefan believed in the pretty lie; the argument would fall on deaf ears. And now he was complacent, too.

"I'll deliver your Seclusion Notice myself. You won't have to debrief with Centurion Darkov before you leave for Wallachia."

All thoughts of Symon's old mortal lover, the child he'd turned against the will of their people, had left him. When he saw Amaranth next, it would be as a sire and a bonded vampire. How strange; his position in vampire society had fallen to the lowest lows, only to rise to its heights.

"Thank you," was all he could manage to say.

In the end, all of his actions before meant nothing if Mildred did not accept him. He refused to carry her away like a Viking. If she rejected him, then Symon would choose madness and death over the alternative.

Stefan would leave with Ness tomorrow night, and Symon would either follow in three days hence, or die in his mate's arms.

# MILDRED

The next morning Mildred found her son in their workroom, scolding his raven. The bird was pecking at Robert's worktable with quick strikes that left dents in the worn wood. Below the bird lay a scattering of walnuts and raw beef, but the raven ignored the food, choosing instead to pulverize it.

"He hasn't eaten anything since yesterday," Robert said, and frowned at his bird. "Can you make him eat, Mother?"

His innocent question brought her up short. Ness was bound for freedom, but the walls of her own cage crept closer day by day. There was nowhere for her to run with Robert where he would be safe. His powers marked him as a monster or a useful pawn for the machinations of the powerful.

Perhaps it was the better fate that his father take him to London early. He would learn to become indispensable, and that would keep him safe even as the tides of magical politics changed.

But what kind of man would Robert become if he embraced his gifts?

"Harry can't eat any more, my dearest." Her voice was gentle as she approached boy and bird, as if either one of them might spook and fly from the room.

"Did I make him sick?" Robert's face scrunched up in tears as he reached out and ran a hand over the bird's head.

The thing that now inhabited the bird's body must have had some access to Harry's memories, because it nuzzled back against Robert's touch just like Harry would have.

Mildred shuddered. Whatever roosted inside the thing was intelligent enough to mimic its host. What else was it capable of?

"Robert, please, you must listen to me."

Her son's face glistened with tears, but he faced her, ready for a lesson that would fix his mistake. Magical knowledge wasn't forgiving, and the lesson she was about to give him would be bitter.

But it was better that he lost his most cherished familiar than his soul. Better to raise a bird from the dead than a person.

"That is no longer Harry." Mildred couldn't bring herself to accuse Robert of killing the animal. It must have been an accident. "The part of Harry that made him your pet left, and something else filled in the empty space. He is not your friend, though he will be loyal to you for as long as you keep him animate."

"He can't be dead! Harry is right here! He's the same bird he's ever been. You're lying!"

She had expected a powerful reaction, but the denial still stung.

"Like people, animals aren't meant to come back from the dead, my dearest. I know you have a wonderful power within you, but you must not use it again. We mages cannot play God. Terrible things happen when we try."

He didn't believe her.

For a moment, she saw a flash of his father in Robert's face; the coldness overtook her sweet boy and then was gone again, as if William Cecil had temporarily possessed his son, just like the infernal creature on the worktable.

"What do you know? You're just a woman," Robert spat at her, and then he ran off.

The raven tilted its had at her and let out a deep, gurgling croak that sounded like underworld laughter. It took off a moment later to follow its master.

Mildred was left alone, wondering if she'd already lost her son.

"I MUST SPEAK WITH YOU, my lord." Mildred found her husband in the study. She did not let her eyes wander to the wine cabinet where he kept his poison, but she sensed the hellebore crystal as she crossed into the room. Was he truly so careless? A servant could find the noxious poison while restocking his wines with ease.

If he did not care who found the poison, then he could not care who he used it on.

"I am not available to discuss matters of the household at this time." He paused and rang the silver bell on his desktop to call a servant in to clear his lunch.

His plate of cold roasted meat and cheese was only picked at. The man had no appetite for food or flesh, as if he were naturally suspicious of all carnal pleasures.

"It is of grave importance. Our son is in danger, that raven —"

Lord Burghley cut her off, rising from his desk with a rare, thin smile.

"It is remarkable, is it not? I have done some reading on the phenomenon. The creature can share its sight with

Robert. Remarkable, just remarkable." He was practically giddy, no doubt thinking of all the spying his son could do for Elizabeth's shadow network of informants.

"It is dangerous. Please, you must listen to reason. Necromancy is infernal magic. The entity that dwells inside the bird is malicious. It could influence Robert in ways we cannot begin to fathom. You must have the thing destroyed."

He laughed at her as he put his cap on and adjusted it in the small mirror behind her. He looked past his wife, as if she were a piece of furniture that had learned to speak at an inconvenient moment.

"Nonsense, woman. Robert's mind is a steel trap. His Latin and rhetoric marks are outstanding. The boy has as strong a mind as I, and he will master the thing without difficulty." He wasn't angry with her, only impatient.

"Now, I must be off to Stamford. The Witch Finder General has taken ill and died, leaving us in a difficult position with a witch at large. I'll be gone three days. When I return, I expect Robert's effects to be in order so we may leave for London at once."

His voice turned cold, and the smile melted from his mouth.

He reached out and gripped Mildred's wrist, squeezing it until her bones creaked. The unexpected and violent contact made her freeze.

"I will not hear another word about Robert's raven or his magical training. These are not decisions for you to make." He released her as if she were an unclean thing and stalked out of the room, his temper soured behind that cold, placid mask.

She walked towards the window and watched as Lord Burghley climbed into a velvet-lined carriage and signaled his footman to drive on. He wasn't above going about in comfort when the eyes of the Court were not present to see his false frugality.

If she were a good mother and a decent woman, Mildred would go and find her son so that she might reason with him, or try to spend the limited time she had remaining with him. But she stood where she was, watching her husband's carriage until it disappeared into wood.

The leaves were turning russet and gold, and Mildred sensed the dying season ravaging the dark forest beyond the estate.

Tonight, she would venture into the wilderness, and there she would sin as sweetly as she dared, for all the touchstones of her godly marriage were crumbling beneath her fingertips.

Maybe in the jaws of a wolf she would find some wisdom in abandon or welcome death.

## SYMON

The confidence he displayed earlier had all but disappeared by the time he crept into the Burghley estate orchard.

It was possible that his sweet mate would hide behind the locked doors and magically sealed threshold of the grand manor house where he couldn't reach her.

He couldn't blame her for doing so. Her husband's spies had spread through the captured lands of Terra Noxa's crusade, feeding the English Crown with torrid stories of the vampire conquest, though not all of them were untrue; the council kept a tight watch over England's Virgin Queen.

Strange that his beautiful wife haunted the dark corridors of this grand estate while Burghley dwelled at court. It was as if Burghley was ashamed of the woman, though Symon could not find fault in her, biased as he was.

Symon guessed that there was no love between Mildred and her husband, but that could very well be wishful thinking on his part. It would be easier to seduce an unhappy woman from a burdensome union than kidnap a powerful baroness with political ties.

Somehow, he doubted she was the latter.

The minutes crawled by as a black raven circled above him. The moon was full enough for Symon to see the back steps of the manor house and the secluded little shadow where he'd kissed her last night.

He almost convinced himself to slink down into the long shadows of the hedges around the back gardens when the door opened and a cloaked figure stepped into the night. Her scent curled in the wind, lighting his loins on fire and fogging his mind.

Her large black cloak caught the autumn breeze and revealed a strip of white fabric so fine it was almost translucent to his eyes.

His fangs dropped, and his cock strained against his leather breeches. He had to reach down to palm himself and hiss into the night before she got too close and their evening was over before it had begun.

Symon would not fail her so quickly; his mate would have the wild hunt her body craved.

He stepped back into the shadows, melding with them perfectly until only the ruby glow of his eyes shone from the darkness. Mildred passed him, the hood of her cloak fallen down to reveal her red hair spilling down in chaotic waves across her back.

He reached out and combed his icy fingers through her sweet, perfumed locks. She gasped and turned, but she was too slow. By the time her gaze swept the apple tree, he was gone.

Her heart sped, filling the orchard with her musical beat. Symon would gladly toy with her until dawn, but his time was better spent at the chase than the tease.

"Brave little rabbit, you came," he whispered as he stepped into the moonlight behind her. The shadow of his breath brushed her neck, and this time he didn't hide when she spun to look at him.

Her scent hit him hard. Arousal, anticipation, and just enough fear to make it all interesting.

"Against my better judgment, yes." Her mouth was a perfect red berry on her face, set in a severe line that failed to hide the hunger in her eyes.

"Reason and judgment are for cowards and scholars." He reached out and curled a strand of her hair around his finger, marveling at the silken caress of it.

"England is full of cowards, Mr. Vitre."

He growled, snapping his free hand out to grip her by the hip and pull her close enough to feel the unreasonable hardness of his britches.

"I am Symon. Do not speak to me like a scraping courtier. My name, and my name alone, will fall from those lips when I chase you down."

He slipped his hand from her hair down into the cloak, skimming his fingers around her sides and back until he palmed the sizable globes of her backside.

She started at the touch but didn't scream or twist away. Mildred leaned closer to him as one of her dainty little hands splayed across his parted lips.

"I want to feel you at my back, I —". She trailed off and shook her head like a drunk too deep in her cups. "Are you going to drink from me, Symon? Is that what happens when you catch me?"

She wanted him so much that she risked his fangs, not knowing what it meant if they sank into her skin. His mate was brave and needy.

Symon pressed her against the trunk of a nearby tree, covering her small, plush body with his sizable bulk as his hands met over her belly and traveled up to cup her weighty breasts.

He swallowed her gasp with a deep, wet kiss and wedged

his thigh between her legs. A pleased growl echoed in her mouth as she ground down against the hard muscle of his leg, her slick cunt soaking them both where they made contact.

"No," he whispered as he pulled back, just enough for his overheated breath to wash over her kiss bruised lips. "I'm going to devour this needy little cunt." He lifted his thigh, and Mildred moaned, her feet kicking as they rose from the ground and all of her weight bore down through her sex against his leg.

"God, help me." She gasped.

Symon gave her a feral, fanged grin and laughed. "God can't save you now. I've got your scent."

Then he was gone, leaving her to collapse against the tree as he melted back into the shadows. He waited for her to catch her breath before filling the night with a howl.

"Time to run, little rabbit."

# MILDRED

The slick of her desire coated her inner thighs as she raced through the forest, heart pumping, sweat plastering her hair to her forehead. She'd never felt so alive. This was the feeling she chased when she slipped into the bodies of rabbits, mice, and foxes.

A heart pounding, connection with her body and the earth that cradled it. To feel as present and ephemeral as an animal.

But she wasn't an animal; she was herself. Lady Burghley, Mildred Cooke, mother and wife. At that moment, she possessed herself completely, and there was a predator at her back who wanted her.

All of her. Every dark, wanton, needful part of her.

Mildred might die tonight. There was every chance that the vampire was lying. But it would be a glorious end, better than wasting away in a dark room and an enormous bed while her grandchildren wept.

Tonight, she might die on her feet, running with her life in her own hands, and it was glorious.

Whatever happened, she knew where she wanted to be

caught, and so she led the vampire deeper into the woods where they had met the night before, toward a place she had spent the darkest moments of her marriage.

As the Rose Grotto came into view, the scent of the late roses that grew at the base of the fountain washed over her senses. She would lead him into the clearing and confront him, just as she had the other night.

Before Mildred could get to the bench, the vampire struck, and she found herself flattened to the cool ground. He was hot against her back and hard where his cock pressed into the flesh of her backside.

She pushed against him, scrambling back up to her hands, unwilling to give in so easily. Before she managed to crawl away, one of his large hands closed over the base of her throat and pulled her back against him.

The steady weight of his grip wasn't enough to restrict her breathing, but it could.

He sat back, kneeling on the ground behind her, and pulled her up so that her legs spread over his thighs and his opposite hand pressed into her belly. He had been cold as death when he touched her hair, but now Symon burned as if a fever was ravaging his body.

Mildred kicked and thrashed, choking herself against his hand as she pushed against him, but she didn't care. Her heart fluttered wildly.

She'd never felt so alive.

"Mm, I do love your spirit, little strawberry," he rumbled into her ear. "But I've got you now, and it's time to feast." The hand on her belly slipped down and cupped her sex through her shift.

She soaked the fabric and seized up, gasping through the hard press of the fingers curled around her throat.

When he'd said he was going to devour her *cunt,* she hadn't quite understood how. Her marriage bed had been a cold, rushed affair. Relations had stopped immediately when Robert was born. Mildred heard whispers of other sexual acts, a godless fornication that vampires no doubt indulged in.

"You're all bark," she rasped, teasing him with a smile.

He growled into her ear and then flipped her onto her back. The movement was violent, yet he was careful not to knock the wind out of her or hit her head too hard on the ground.

His pale hands moved so fast that they blurred in the night as they unhooked the clasp of her cloak and pulled her nightgown from her body. A loud rip echoed through the grotto like cannon shot, but she didn't care what the laundress would think tomorrow morning when she took Mildred's washing.

The vampire spread her legs wide but didn't move any further. The dark shadow of his body covered her pale flesh, and his red gaze roamed over the soft divots and mounds of her flesh, his red eyes glinting with greed and rapacious desire.

The cool air lashed against the damp curls of her sex as he gripped her thighs. The vampire hooked her knees up and over his shoulders and then leaned down. There were no gentle kisses or searching touches against her skin. The only warning she received was a wash of his hot breath over her cunt before his tongue delved between her lips.

His massive body flattened against her, one hand gripping her thigh so hard the soft flesh dented around his fingers; the other hand held her bucking hips down against the ground so she could do nothing but writhe as he lapped at her sex.

God, he was *eating* her like a starved beast.

It was divine and degenerate and perfect.

His hot tongue circled that little pearl of nerves in her sex that her own clumsy explorations had teased at. Now it came alive with a jolt of pleasure so powerful her thighs shook against his ears. He pressed the flat of his tongue against it and then took the little bud gingerly between his sharp teeth, forcing a wail of delight to fill the grotto.

Mildred arched her back up off the ground and dug her nails into the earth to feel her grounding pulse.

Another wild moan filled the air when Symon replaced his tongue with the pad of his thumb and played quick circles over the worried flesh of her nub. Her skin was glistening with sweat as her body churned for him, and yet she wasn't prepared for the intrusion of his tongue into her tight channel.

He filled her and played her at the same time with that wet, thick muscle, just as strong as the rest of his impossibly powerful body. The scrape of his fangs shot little curls of pain to heighten the unrelenting pleasure coiling her belly. Her body was priming itself, ready to spring like a coil at any moment.

That moment came when she felt his tongue curl inside of her and press hard at some unknown secret in her channel. A rush of her wet pleasure washed over his face as her release hit her like a bolt of lightning, seizing up her muscles and heightening the tremors in her legs and belly.

Mildred's breath came hard and fast as Symon guided her through the aftershocks of her release. The heat that built up between them was like a balm over her tight muscles as they slowly released and her body fell back against her sweat soaked cloak.

Everything in nature witnessed and rejoiced. It felt like the earth herself cradled them in that moment as Mildred's senses settled back into her ravaged body. Never in her life had she felt so thoroughly run through, and so well-paced.

The warm weight of her vampire crawled up her body, shielding her from the chill in the night with his heated skin and soft jerkin. His firm cock pressed against her wet, shivering cunt lips as he settled over her, but he made no move to release himself or demand that she reciprocate.

He pinned her to the earth. It made her feel held and safe, and not trapped.

Symon rumbled contentedly, as if he'd just found his satisfaction, and she ran her fingers through the shock of white hair on his head, marveling at the way he nuzzled against her, the same as he had done in the body of a wolf last night.

"Are you satisfied now that you've captured your prey?" Mildred asked softly.

An unnatural predator pinned her down and curled around her, and yet she felt no fear of him. The hazy aftermath of her pleasure had obliterated her earlier worries. A small voice inside of her warned that she shouldn't be complacent, but it was difficult to focus on with his steady warm bulk on top of her.

"I will never be satisfied with you, little strawberry." His rough words rumbled through her chest where they pressed against one another.

Symon's confession filled her with the most delicious tremor of fear, but she couldn't do anything but bask in the light of his desire.

He pulled his head up and away from where it lay between her pale breasts and kissed her, forcing Mildred to share the taste of herself. She didn't flinch away but reveled in the earthen flavor of his sharp mouth and her sex. When he pulled back, that ruby gaze settled on her neck.

"You have fed a beast who will forever beg at your door for what scraps you give him." he whispered, and pressed his forehead against hers. "Please forgive me for all that I will do, though I do not deserve it."

Fear slammed into her, his confession finally pulling her

out of her bliss. Her muscles came back to life with tension and dynamic action, but before she could shove him away from her, the vampire was gone, melded back into the shadows, moving too fast for her mortal eyes to detect in the half light.

Mildred didn't linger long enough to ponder his cryptic words, not with the weight of an unknown predator watching her from the shadows. He had chased her into the grotto, and now it seemed he would guide her back home.

She tried to ignore the sense of foreboding that built inside her as she slipped her shift back on and pulled her cloak tight around her body. By the time she made it to the back door, her pulse was high in her throat and her body slicked with sweat.

Her vampire had given Mildred the chase she desired, but she didn't know if he intended to let her go after catching her.

# SYMON

The necessity of his species' deception and seduction of their rare-bloods made more sense in hindsight. How could Mildred understand the need he felt for her until he fed her his cock and drank from her neck?

When he completed their bond, she would feel the depth of his ache for her, but giving her his kiss and taking her without telling her what it meant for the rest of their long lives together was diabolical.

Symon was unsure if he could do it honestly. He'd witnessed months-long courtships in their conquered lands and sweet love matches formed, but he couldn't hope to give Mildred the comfort of time.

He was an enemy to England and her own husband's government; extending his courtship was madness. Not to mention the danger Lord Burghley posed to her directly.

His encounter with Mildred had not taken the entire evening, and he had many hours to spend before daylight poisoned the sky. Once he made sure she was tucked safely within the mansion, he shifted into his wolf skin and bounded into the night.

Symon covered vast distances in a tenth of the time it took a fully rested horse to travel; and he was motivated to be swift that evening.

When he arrived in Stamford, Symon spent the rest of the evening shadowing his mate's husband. He had his own spies and had them running in the daylight. Mildred's husband had traveled to Stamford, where the sheriff and the Witch Finder administered what they called justice for the entire county.

Symon would have hated the man regardless; but Lord Burghley's suspicious activities filled him with cold dread and hot malice.

The Lord was staying at the house of Stamford's sheriff, which was easily the finest and most imposing structure in the small village surrounded by a high dry rock wall and dense hedges. The mortals within paid no mind to the sleek, invisible form of his wolf, and the wattle and daub walls failed to mute the conversation that took place inside.

A dozen heartbeats pounded through the walls, but it didn't take Symon long to sniff out the stale scent that haunted the Burghley estate. He crept around the back of the house and curled his wolf-sized body below a jutting casement window where he could hear the hearts of two men, one beating fast with anxiety, the other slow like a lizard warming on a rock.

"It is a difficult task, my Lord, to organize the shire's militia without our Witch Finder." A nasally voice spoke; it belong to the man with the rabbiting heart Symon assumed was the sheriff.

"Unacceptable. This is why we need to train more of the gentry up as Witch Finders. There should be ten for every hundred thousand people." The steady, cold voice was punctuated by the scratch of a quill against paper, as if he were taking notes on how best to oppress his people.

"That could take decades, lord, and I fear the Tansy girl will be gone by then." A long silence stretched, and Symon scented both fear and the icy tang of disgust.

"Oh?" Symon had never met Lord Burghley, but his voice was exactly as imagined, somehow dismissive in one breath and commanding in the other. As if his orders had already been followed.

"The ports, they are difficult to monitor, and there are miles of shore. The witch would need a great deal of coin to book passage, but that is the only way she could—"

Something cut the man off. Burghley had not touched the man, but he might as well have slapped him for the uptick in the other sheriff's pulse.

"Where could she obtain so large a sum, and so quickly?" The lord's question was rhetorical. Symon had seen the state of the girl's clothes and the roughness of her hands; not even her prosperous father had made enough money to pay for half the passage on a merchant vessel.

No doubt Lord Burghley had come to the same conclusion.

"Fetch me a scrying mirror. I must send a message to my clerk in London immediately." The lord's tone was measured, and yet the second heartbeat in the room battered its rib cage, fulfilling his request.

Symon had heard enough. He ran from his hiding place and into the little village, thinking it was good that Stefan and the mortal mage were long gone from England by then. Burghley could not know that vampires were interfering in his persecution, but now his suspicions had turned to his wife: the only person who both knew the Tansy child and had the means to aid her.

Symon shifted into the form of a bat, not his favorite skin to wear, but it was much less conspicuous than a wolf prowling a land that had eradicated them generations ago.

He flitted about town, stopping first at the inn to listen in on the nightly gossip. Stamford's meager tavern was serving as a makeshift mourning party for a group of young men deep in their cups. The small, black bat hung himself on the thatched eave just outside the window and trained his ears to pick up the conversation at the nearest table.

"I'll have another, for Master Boswick! Dead in his bed!" a drunken young man slurred, knocking over a half full flagon of stale cider. One of his companions slapped him down, and the inebriated man collapsed onto the table.

"And three good men in our company, torn to shreds the night before. There are devils in England!" another man, drunk and half-dressed in armor, shouted.

An older woman with a dirty white coif covering thin gray hair delivered another round of cups to the loud mourners.

"Drink up, his lordship's paying the tab tonight," she said, slapping one man hard on the back to keep him from falling over. "But don't make too much of a fuss. Your master's death was awfully sudden, wasn't it? That witch you lot failed to catch gave him the eye, I know it," the old woman whispered to the men, delighting in the horror that washed over their drunken faces.

Symon doubted Ness had time to curse the Witch Finder General on her way out of the country with Stefan, but it was strange that Boswick had died so suddenly.

He got his answer in the Boswick household an hour later as he crawled in through the attic. He'd shifted back into a man, preferring hands to paw or wing as he slipped through the shadows.

Dry, theatric sobs echoed through the fine home. The lady of the house was in the kitchen, crying over a slab of roasted meat while three small children ran underfoot. He passed the small family and continued into their dining room, where the body of Witch Finder Boswick lay in a narrow wood coffin.

Two candles burned on either end of his body, spelled by a fire elemest to ward off evil smells from wafting off the inert flesh. It did nothing to soften the stink of the corpse for Symon, but he'd smelled far worse on battlefields and in churches.

There was one scent that stood out against the decaying flesh of the Witch Finder, though.

Hellebore crystal. Enough to liquefy his organs and kill the man so painfully that despite the white kerchief tied under his jaw, his mouth was mangled in a mask of final agony.

He stood there for a moment as the puzzle pieces took shape in his mind. There was only one way to confirm his suspicions, and it would require he enter Burghley House.

Though he did not know if he could keep his hands off its mistress long enough to confirm his deadly suspicions, he had to try.

If he were right, his mate was in grave danger.

# SYMON

Mortals and immortals alike shared the common desire to cover their mistakes and weaknesses. A man like Lord Burghley, a baron with a title freshly minted by his Virgin Queen, would go to great lengths to protect his reputation. How far he would go depended on the man's ruthlessness and how much he stood to lose from the fickle court of their young queen.

Daylight threatened to pierce the sky, but Symon couldn't rest until he knew what Burghley's involvement was for certain. It was not a great leap from poisoning a disappointing lackey to a wife. The man hadn't touched Mildred in years. No scent of passion or affection lingered on her skin. A man who could spend years away from that sweet strawberry bed was a cold-hearted bastard indeed.

The sky heated above Symon as he slipped into the shadows of the servant's entrance and wove his way through a daisy chain of darkness. The house stirred as he moved past carpeted halls, groggy scullery maids and porters lighting the first of the day's fires.

His beast gnashed inside him, clawing at his skin when he reached the second floor.

Symon's instincts urged him to follow that sweet strawberry scent, but his rational mind had locked onto the potent poisonous aroma of hellebore, and he couldn't lose the thread. It was the same poison that slowly pickled Boswick's corpse, and once he found it, then he could decide what was to be done about his mate.

There was death in the manor, too.

It was small and new, but the whiff of the infernal flowed through it. Like most vermin, a necromancer's lair developed a distinct stench of its own that warded off lesser predators. Was Lord Burghley a death-speaker? Terra Noxa's intelligence on Elizabeth and her Privy Councilors hadn't mentioned the Secretary of State possessing any magic at all.

It couldn't be Mildred. Her magic was pure and pagan, as alive and vital as the woman herself.

Intriguing as the mystery was, Symon couldn't afford to investigate. He would deal with whatever undead thing stalked these halls when it became a problem. That hyper focused predator within him was good for some things, and forcing him to maintain his focus was one of its few benefits.

Soft footfalls dampened by the drag of long velvet prickled his ears from behind him. Mildred's scent hit him first, followed by the low tones of her panicked voice as she spoke to the woman with the weak heartbeat next to her. He blended into a shadowed alcove as they passed, resisting the gut wrenching urge to reach out and run his fingers through her wild red hair.

It remained undone and tangled from when he had left her on the forest floor hours earlier.

"What am I to tell the cook, mistress? A dressed peacock does not get up and wander out into the vegetable garden." The woman, a servant most likely, whispered sharply.

"Tell him that the lady of the house has a distaste for the meat and you got rid of it. If he has anything else to say, he can say it to me directly," Mildred said. The sweet breath of her words tickled his face as the woman passed him completely and disappeared up another flight of stairs.

Whatever mischief that was, it would have to wait. More necromantic devilry, no doubt.

Luckily, the hellebore scent concentrated in the room at the end of the hall. In his haste, Symon dropped the pretense of stealth entirely and entered through the door. He should have left the house and then crept back in through a window now that he knew where the room was, but he was in too much of a hurry and too focused on his mission to be cautious.

The stink of poison was easy to pinpoint, and so was the delivery method. Symon found two empty wine cups at the lord's wine cabinet. Someone had cleaned the silver cups, but not well enough to remove all the traces of hellebore to his nose. Even more damning was the pouch he found behind a secret latch at the back of the cabinet.

He brushed his fingers over it and felt nothing, though he knew it had to be enchanted to work so devastatingly well on a full-grown man.

The confirmation of his suspicions gripped his heart with fear.

"You shouldn't be here, vampire," Mildred whispered.

He turned to where she stood in the doorway, a candle held in one hand as she closed the study door behind them with the other. She was beautiful in her crimson dressing gown, but she'd washed the brand of his tongue and her pleasure from between her legs. A dark, territorial part of his soul wanted to pin her down and ravage her all over again, take her deeper, harder, in a way she'd never be able to wash away.

Symon shook his head like a dog and bared his teeth. “Not many can sneak up on me; I’m impressed.”

Her smile was beatific, tugging at her lips as if they’d almost forgotten how to curl up with joy. “The house and the stones love me,” she said.

“Not enough to protect you from this,” he said, and held up the pouch containing the hellebore. “But you can see it, can’t you, with your mage-sight?”

She nodded solemnly. Symon guessed she was powerful, but there were few earth elemests who would fail to see the toxic glow of poison, even through fabric.

“I saw it happen last night when we returned. The lord doesn’t know, don’t worry.”

He must have been losing his touch if she could detect his raw emotions on his face, or perhaps it was fitting that she was the only person in the world who could.

“You will be next. He already suspects that you aided Ness,” he said as he placed the pouch back in its secret resting place. He didn’t want the lord to use the pouch’s contents on his mate, but he couldn’t risk alerting Cecil to the discovery of his activities.

“I’m the mother of his heir,” she whispered, but it was a weak argument, even to herself.

“Come with me to Flanders. There will be a boat in two nights time.” He hadn’t meant to reveal his plan to her yet, but the mounting danger forced his hand.

“I can’t leave my son with that man. You have no idea what he has planned for him.” Her voice shook, and Symon could only imagine. He’d had no children in mortal life, and his recent siring hung on him in thick ropes of shame.

He took a step toward her and tilted her chin up. “Your son is responsible for the peacock, isn’t he?”

Mildred’s eyes went glassy, shining with tears as her breath caught. “Lord Burghley wants to use Robert’s power for the Crown. He wants to *nurture* the darkness in our son. I can't abandon him now. We must bring him with us."

Symon could not offer her comfort, only safety.

"Terra Noxa is at war. A battlefront is no place for a child, let alone the child of Elizabeth's lapdog. I can't stop my people from using him as a pawn, or worse. We do not tolerate necromancy. Our own witches would kill him."

And Symon wouldn't question their wisdom. Necromancers were a plague on the living and the undead.

The first of her Mildred's desperate sobs sounded in the room as the chime of day bells rang through his mind. The sun was rising, and he was fast running out of time.

"I must go, but I will return tomorrow night. Meet me in the wood, or hide. It matters not. I will find you wherever you go." He sealed his dark promise with a gentle kiss and left her there, the sun at his heels as he raced through the shortening shadows of the forest to bed down for the night in the den of a fox.

# MILDRED

A low, white mist crept along the damp green clearing of the grotto. Mildred paced, her bare feet cold as icicles as she wore a track between the bench and the rose scented fountain.

She had no doubt that her husband would poison her as readily as the greedy Witch Finder General, but she could easily detect the poison. A shudder worked through her body as she wondered what other methods he would attempt when poison proved to be ineffective against an earth elemest.

"You're shivering, little strawberry." Symon appeared behind her, as if he'd been born whole from the darkness between the leaves above.

She spun around as he advanced on her, crowding her through the mist until the backs of her knees hit the cold stone bench. His hands came up to rest over her shoulders. The heat from his splayed fingers sunk down into her muscles and loosened the tension she hadn't known she was carrying.

He dropped to his knees before her. No sweet words, no

seduction, only the beautiful hell of his red eyes like stoked embers in the silver gloom of the deep night.

"I feel cold in my bones, like the clay of the grave," Mildred whispered as she leaned against him and pressed her forehead against the crown of his head.

"This could be my death, but I want to taste every morsel of life before it ends."

He parted the folds of her cloak and slipped his hands under the hem of her shift. Those warm, rough fingers skimmed over her calves, then hooked between her thighs to part them. "Death is a choice. You can choose this—" One of his thumbs flicked between her slick petals and rubbed against her sore little bud. "I can give you endless nights of pleasure and days of unending freedom."

She bucked against his hand, even as she denied him. "I have too much to lose," she gasped as he filled her with two thick fingers. He captured her mouth in a kiss, worrying her lips with his sharp fangs and invading her mouth with his searching tongue.

"Do you?" Symon asked as his mouth chased and caught her own. "What do you truly own in that tomb of a house?" He plunged his tongue into her throat before she could answer him.

Symone pulled away from her. The hot, wet brand of his mouth joined his fingers as he pumped into her. The flat of his tongue beat a quick, lazy staccato against her pearl as she writhed. That heavy, delicious tension began to tangle up into coils in her lower belly as she leaned back.

What did she truly own? Her body had been bartered, bred and then put on a shelf; only the memory of sensations remained. The sun warmed scent of green hay, the quick beat of a humming bird's heart and the taste berries stolen from the bramble.

The mass of her shift and her pale thighs obscured the work

of his tongue and fingers, but that stripe of silver white hair on his head glinted in the moonlight. Mildred gripped him there, pulling his face hard into her sex as she moved against him.

She was close to coming undone and losing all sense of herself. But she wanted more than his wicked mouth and his probing fingers.

Mildred moaned and then whimpered, pulling away with panting, desperate breaths. "Stop."

He heeded her command, but reluctantly. When the vampire pulled his fingers from her clenching body, he curled them up to play with the sensitive buttons within, forcing her to shiver as he released her.

She pushed him onto his back. Symon went down easy for her with a surprised grin on his fanged mouth. "As you command, my lady," he said with a breathy growl.

"Show me what you have, sir," Mildred whispered, and reached down to worm her fingers into the ties of his breeches. She knew he was big, but she hadn't seen him fully erect, and his length shocked her. When she pressed her hand against it, he groaned and thrust into her grip, but just as she was about to free her prize, he stopped her.

"If we go further down this road, there's no returning." The playfulness in his face was gone, replaced with the deathly stillness of his predatory heart.

"I don't understand. Can you get me with child?"

He shook his head, a rueful smile playing on his lips that didn't reach his eyes. "No—"

He pulled her clothing off with quick hands while she straddled his legs and palmed her heavy breasts. "No, there can be no children."

The conflicting sensation of his heated palms and the cool night air made her belly clench and her back arch as she ground her core down against his thigh.

"It is a bond, a pact between our bodies. We will crave one another, and you will be my companion through the long night." His voice struggled to rise above a whisper as they stared down at one another. She didn't understand quite what he meant, and it seemed like he didn't have the words to articulate it in a way she understood.

"Is it a marriage? I have had enough of that in this life."

Even as she said it, she knew she was wrong. Mildred would become this strange creature's bride, damn what that would mean for her own soul.

"It is more than that. The ancient pact is sealed by our joining —" he opened his mouth and growled like a starved wolf "and my fangs in your neck. I don't know if I can stop this." He panted and writhed as her slender fingers gripped him.

She watched, awed, as the swipe of her thumb over his glistening cock head made the vampire yelp and whimper. Mildred wanted him. She wanted to watch this creature with all the power of shadow and fang come undone by her and her alone.

"I'll take the chance to have you," she confessed in a breathy whisper. She would have one thing that was hers alone, which no one could take from her after the fact.

Her father had chosen her husband, her husband would take her son, and perhaps her life. In the end, she truly owned nothing but her own desire. Mildred's choice risked her immortal soul and the small family she'd sheltered within the cold halls of Burghley House. But that life was only borrowed; a capricious whim or a cold suspicion could shatter it.

Death loomed as the final chapter to all love stories and it would be no different for this brief interlude with Symon. Let him sink his teeth and his cock into her flesh; Mildred would ride both until they were both satisfied and relish in the last choice afforded her.

The world tumbled and blurred as he moved beneath her and positioned Mildred on her hands and knees. The hot, fevered press of his bare chest branded her back as he draped himself against her. At some point, he had shed his own clothing, but he'd moved too fast for her to see how.

Mildred's knees dug into the cold, wet ground, and her fingers clawed against the earth. She felt the anticipation of infinitely small, furred beings who had presented themselves in a similar posture.

He was going to have her like an animal, and she wanted it too.

"Spread your knees out for me, strawberry." His wicked breath curled against her ear from behind as she obeyed his command and widened her kneeling stance against the ground.

She must not have widened herself for him enough, because his powerful hands spread her wide enough to part her wet, glistening folds against the cold night. A steady hand pressed her face into the grass, and she felt herself open even more.

Symon exposed her so completely that she could feel his eyes drinking in the gentle pink of her inner thighs and wet petals.

"Fuck," he whispered, like a prayer, and swiped his hand through the thick honey that steadily slipped from her sex. "Are you comfortable? I hope so, because I don't think I'll ever let you move. Gods, you're perfect." His big, rough hand palmed the globe of her backside, and she found her impatience begin to overtake the anticipation of the moment.

"Are you going to admire it all night, or take it?" Mildred gasped as he notched the broad head of his cock against her entrance.

"I thought you might want it slow at first, but I believe I was wrong." He gripped her by the shoulder with one hand and the dip of her thigh with the other.

"I want it like a beast," she said, and whatever else she had intended to say died in her throat as he thrust into her, so deep and thick that her eyes watered from the stretch of him.

"Cry mercy…if you want any," he hissed through clenched teeth. A tremor ran through his hand as his fingers dug sweet bruises into her shoulder. She would delight in carrying the mark of his need through the day like a talisman.

Symon pulled his hips away and dragged the thick length of his cock through her over-heated walls slowly. She felt his absence like a weight before he plunged back into her, clapping his thighs against her round backside and forcing her body to undulate with his stroke.

She was about to accuse him of not delivering on his savage promise when the full weight of his body bore down on her and his hips began a punishing staccato of strikes against her flesh.

The skin on the back of her thighs was red and stinging as he fucked into her, smothering her plush, petite body with his endless hard planes. There was no finesse to his strokes. He slammed into her cunt hard and desperate, as if they were the last of their kind and he had a primordial need to fill her with young.

He was too long and thick to use her so recklessly, but Mildred delighted in the sting that soon turned into mindless rutting pleasure. Her inner muscles gripped and spasmed around him as her thighs and calves clenched, body shaking with an undeniable roil of sensation that began in her cunt but radiated outwards to strangle her breath.

A strange sound joined the rhythmic slap of his hips to her backside, and it took her a few moments to realize that it was the clap of her breasts against her ribs as he fucked her hard enough to violently shake her entire body.

The cold encounters in her marriage bed had been brief and formal, but Symon kept her on her knees as minutes melted into one another and time ceased to mean anything to either of them. The clenching ache of her muscles and her bones intensified as her pleasure crested.

"I know you're close," he bit out, and leaned back. Mildred felt his cock slip from her sore channel completely, which sent a desperate, keening whimper from her mouth at the loss of his hard heat.

He pulled her up from her knees and pressed her against his chest, her legs splayed open over his thighs. Before she could protest, he thrust back into her, anchoring her in place with one hand hooked around her front so that his splayed fingers dug into the soft flesh of her belly and the other palmed her breast.

The angle and the addition of her body weight allowed her to sink down lower onto his cock-head and feel it wedge deeper into her cunt.

When he found her end, her toes curled as he went to work, stretching her on his cock and bouncing her in his lap, her pale body glowing in the wane light of the moon while the dark forest looked on.

Her red hair matted and curled against her forehead as she clenched and shuddered; her body was a spring about to release.

"Could you grow to love this beast?" His breathless whispers crashed into her awareness as he worked her, pace quickening as they slammed together. He undid her mind until the only thing that remained of her was as much animal as he was.

"Yes," she confessed. They didn't know one another, but

she wanted to know him, wanted to plunge her hands into his dark, wild chest and look for whatever heart beat within.

"Then you will forgive me, I hope." His voice was tight with pleasure, effort, and a hint of regret, but there was no time for fear to grow between them.

No room for thoughts, fears, or regrets as she came on his merciless cock, clenching against him and washing both their thighs with a thick flood of her honey.

Mildred threw her head back and screamed into the night like an animal reborn as pleasure so sharp it echoed like pain quickened her body.

He followed after her, quickening her tight channel with his scorching hot seed. No sooner had he spent inside her than her magic pulsed, filling her vision with multi-colored starbursts. Mildred's awareness of the forest contracted until it felt like the whole world was contained between the hard beats of her heart and then expanded out to curl around Symon.

She felt him settle down into her bones, deep where the roots of her being fed off of her blood like an eternal spring. She felt safe and powerful, more animal than woman.

The sensation felt so achingly right that she wondered if this was what she had been aimlessly seeking when she took the form of small prey animals and bounded through the night.

It all happened in a moment, and it was so crushingly beautiful that she felt tears slip down her cheeks. Mildred wanted to tell him that it was perfect, that she had never been so happy to be tethered to another.

Then her senses filled with the harsh growl of his wolf, and that peace shattered as he bit into her neck.

The pain was sharp. It forced her to seize up on his cock and shudder, but soon afterward a dreamy sluggishness filled her limbs. Something locked between them, like the echo of death's boundary slamming shut.

He drank from her for a few moments, but those syrupy seconds were divine. When Symon pulled away to run a tongue over her tender wound, she would have collapsed if not for the immovable cage of his arms around her.

Mildred bobbed in and out of wakefulness and didn't come back to her faculties for what felt like hours. When the euphoric stupor finally lifted, she found herself in a warm, soft embrace, tucked up against Symon, glorious and unabashedly nude.

They were lying on top of her cloak as he idly stroked his hands through her hair. For a few moments, she felt a deep satisfaction that wasn't quite her own and a focused worry that didn't fit in her mind.

"You slept for a few hours, but sunrise is still a long way off." Symon nuzzled her like a wolf cub, running the prickly scruff of his short stubble against her shoulder. He was marking her with his scent, as if they had mated for life.

"I feel different, strange," she confessed, and a dark look passed over Symon's ruby eyes. Before they had fallen together in the dirt like animals, she might have struggled to read that look, but somehow she knew it was guilt. Mildred felt it as keenly as if she were ashamed of something, too.

"You are different, my love." He kissed her, and when their lips parted, he told her how his life was now entwined with her own.

Forever.

# SYMON

Her anger was like a lash made of sunlight, a terrible weapon crafted for him alone. Symon knew what it meant to be mated, but he'd had no idea that he would feel her emotions so vividly.

It was horrific and wondrous at the same time.

"You tricked me!" Mildred pushed him away, her feet slipping against the cold, wet ground as she tried to stand up too quickly. He didn't want to touch her when she wanted to be rid of him, but he lunged to catch her in his arms before his mate fell to the cold ground.

He held her as she beat at his shoulders, her body wracked with sobs as she buried her head into his neck.

Symon didn't deserve this beautiful, wild creature, this woman filled with passion and fire, with the steadiness of the good earth and all its plenty. But that did not mean he would not take her and strive every day to be worthy of the mate he'd never expected to find.

He might have fallen into despair if not for the conflicting emotions washing through his heart.

Anger, desire, and despair.

No hatred, though. Despite her protests, she did not hate him, and Symon didn't know if that made the guilt of what he'd done worse or not.

"I tried to tell you —" He stopped himself, unwilling to lie to her, too.

"Our souls are bound forever; I can feel you in my heart like a shadow." Her tears were hot as they stung his bare neck, and he prayed to the Gods of Shadow and Night that he could take it back, but it was no use.

He had drawn her in, unwittingly snared by the oldest ritual among the vampires of Terra Noxa. She might have been a human ignorant of the particulars of vampire customs, but he knew she could feel the invisible string that tied their hearts together.

"I told you I was a beast." His voice sounded raw to his own ears, thick with the loathing he felt down to the root of himself.

"I thought I understood, but nothing could have prepared me, could it? Tell me, am I the latest in a string of conquests?"

The accusation in her voice stung, as if there could be any other in this life or the next for him.

Mildred flinched as the nauseating recoil of such a thought brushed against her mind. At least this conversation would be clear, no matter how painful it was. He was now incapable of lying to her.

"There is no other person in the world as precious to me now. No man or woman as beautiful, no mind as beguiling. You are the beginning and end of my need."

She shuddered against him as the truth of his confession snared her.

Undying devotion wasn't enough. It could never replace the mortal life he'd ripped from her, but it was the bare minimum, a duty he would give his life to uphold.

"What would happen if I ran from you? If I called in the

Magi from Court and all the fire elemests of England to banish you?"

She did not want to do that; he could feel her anxiety at the prospect of leaving him, even now, but her question was fair.

She wanted to know how long the leash was between them.

"I would die. I need you like the seed needs sun; I will wither away without you." There was no soft way to communicate their bond, but he wouldn't let her believe Symon held all the power. "Our bond is fresh. You would most likely live long after I."

"I wanted something of my own," she murmured to herself, and though he could not sense the exact meaning, he understood the feelings wrapped around it.

Fear, regret, and an immense relief followed by guilt to rival his own.

His poor mate was drowning in the crush of her swirling emotions. Symon held her tightly against him, grateful when she leaned into his touch rather than pull away. A warm blanket of comfort fell over their shoulders as they shared one another's peace.

"I regret how this happened, but I will never regret that I did it. In the eyes of Terra Noxa, my people, you are now Mildred Vitre, and the vows of your mortal life are now severed."

He braced himself for more angry accusations from her, but they didn't come; instead, she was resigned and heartbroken.

"I want to go with you and make a life on my own terms, but I cannot abandon my son." Her desire and her duty to her child would tear his mate apart.

Symon would not let that happen.

"You cannot stay here, Mildred. There is life with me in

Europe, but you will find nothing but death in Burghley House."

She shook her head. "Then Robert will be lost! Better I stay and die at the hands of Lord Burghley than leave him to that. At least he would have a few pure, precious memories of his mother to cling to when he is sent to London and his powers are exploited."

Symon growled, "You are more than a 'pure and precious' symbol of man's salvation, Mildred. I know you raised your son with all the good intentions you posses, but his choices as a man will be his own. Do not think to martyr yourself in the hope you can alter his destiny."

Not even a mother's love could stand in the face of destiny. The boy had been born with powers that made him exploitable in a country hell-bent on power at any cost. England would soon become like Spain, terrorizing the New World and extracting treasure from distant shores the way his own people drank blood from mortal veins.

It was too easy to fall into the seductive power and momentum of conquest, but doing so was nevertheless unforgivable.

"How can I make this decision? I cannot, I am not strong enough." She wept into his chest, and as he held her, a terrible resolve filled him.

"Then I shall take the burden of choice away from you," he whispered in her fragrant red hair, perfumed with the ripeness of summer strawberries.

His mate was kindness; she was the fecund bounty of a high summer harvest, and her heart was the truest he had ever known.

He would not let her suffer this alone. Symon would gladly be Mildred's villain if it set her free.

# MILDRED

Mildred stood at the casement window in the library, watching the sunset on the third night of Lord Burghley's absence.

She was out of time, but she couldn't help but linger to watch the white gravel road that led to the manor, her fingers toying with the silver pomegranate pomander dangling from her girdle.

The soft clatter of the long dried pomegranate seeds reminded her of the words Symon left her with the night before.

*"I do not ask for your trust; it is not a gift I have earned. But know that I will take you, and keep you, and none in your household will ever believe you came with me willingly."*

Mildred couldn't guess what he meant, but she prepared herself for the inevitable by wearing her favorite jewels and hiding a bound book of Robert's first letters in her pocket. She was a rich woman, but if she was to flee her former life in the dead of night like a thief, she was determined to only take the things that were most precious to her: a ring given to her by her sister the summer she died, her mother's favorite pearl necklace, letters written in a child's unsteady hand, and an old silver pomander that was long out of fashion, treasures her husband often scoffed at and forbade her from wearing to court, for they were 'cheap ornaments' in the eyes of the courtiers among whom he curried favor.

Burghley could keep her fine gowns and her heavy gold brooches, give them to the next unsuspecting woman caught in his web.

A plume of white dust caught the fading rays of the sun as the dark outline of Lord Burghley's carriage made its progress down the drive and stopped in front of the great oaken door of Burghley House.

Mildred leaned against the dark, wood-paneled wall and asked the ancient stones for strength. Her pagan prayers were heresy, but they gave her more comfort than the dead wood pulp of her Bible. The stones answered her, whispering of fire from the belly of the earth, or endless smoothing rain and the powerful crack of thunder.

In the end Mildred was nothing in the face of what was primordial, and so was Lord Burghley. That gave her a strange measure of strength as she turned away from the window.

The heavy door groaned on its hinges as a small shadow cast into the room. Robert stood with one hand on the heavy brass handle and the other holding Lord Burghley's copy of *Le Morte d'Arthur,* which she had been reading with her son for almost a year. Her heart clenched as he crept into the room, his quiet anticipation palpable.

Robert loved the stories of Arthur and his Round Table, and she thought the tales of brave men and their good deeds were better teachers of virtue than Bible stories. The knowledge that tonight would be their last time reading by the fire strengthened her resolve.

"Is it time to return to Camelot so soon, dearest?"

Mildred said, the calm of the stones overtaking her as she settled herself in the high-backed chair situated in front of the hearth.

"Yes. Father will be home soon, won't he?" Robert padded forward and took a seat on the carpeted floor before handing the worn cloth covered book to her. Mildred and her son had an unspoken agreement not to read when Lord Burghley was in residence. He thought fairy tales and stories of knightly intrigue to be beneath the interest of his only son.

But Mildred would not pretend to read from the Book of Common Prayer on what were likely her last few moments with her son.

"He will, but never you mind that. He will be occupied in the stables and with Mortly for a while. Let's see…we left off with Isolde and Tristan, I believe." A green ribbon marked their progress, chapter twenty-four, wherein Isolde and Tristan mistakenly drink the love potion meant for Isolde's wedding night.

*"'Then they laughed and made good cheer, and either drank to the other freely, and they thought never drink that ever they drank to other was so sweet nor so good.'"* Her voice was clear and even as she read out from the small, primitive typeset.

Before she could finish the paragraph, a dark form slipped into the library through the heavy doors. Mildred looked up, her hands shaking so badly that she nearly dropped the book. Her heart pounded so loud she heard it like a crashing wave in her own throat, and for a moment she thought Symon had chosen his moment and come too soon, before she could wring her last precious moments with her son.

Her heart sank into her stomach when she saw that it was Lord Burghley, wearing his heavy traveler's cloak and looking as severe as an old saint's statue.

"Reading romance by the light of the fire, I see." His face

broke into a brittle smile that he directed at Robert. The boy reflected that false light and bathed in it.

"Can we finish the chapter, please, Father? I've been very good at my studies and my tutors are all best pleased."

Burghley pretended indulgence and stepped closer toward the fire.

In his hand, he carried one of the wineglasses he kept in his study, perhaps the same glass he'd used to deliver the hellebore crystal to Boswick. The evil glow radiating from the rim told her that it didn't need to be the same cup. He'd slipped the poison in, knowing that she could see it as clearly.

The book fell to the floor at her skirts, and Robert scrambled to pick it up while Lord Burghley set the cup on the table next to Mildred. His voice was low and emotionless when he leaned in to whisper, "Drink it, and your son will not know that you are a traitor and a liar."

No grand speech, no accusation, just another command he expected her to obey without question. Then he turned and fixed Robert with another indulgent smile.

"Of course, but don't tarry too long. Your mother is tired and needs a long rest." Then he turned and left, disappearing silently out the door without a backward glance.

"Thank you!" Robert called after his father, and then insistently placed the book back in Mildred's shaking hands. She stared down at her son and then glanced at the goblet of wine, the sick green aura of the hellebore curling into the air above the rim like rotten smoke.

Her calm came back to her, and she opened the book, reading the rest of the words out loud like a prayer.

*"'But by that their drink was in their bodies, they loved either other so well that never their love departed for weal neither for woe. And thus it happed the love first betwixt Sir Tristram and La Beale Isoud, the which love never departed the days of their life.'"*

She had drunk love like poison from Symon Vitre, and like Isolde she would never be the same; it could not be separated from her blood or vein.

As she smiled down at Robert, she asked herself again, was it better to die with her son's love than to risk it and live?

In that split second, before it all happened, she had her answer.

She took the wine goblet and flung the contents into the fire. The flames burned emerald green and leapt from the hearth so violently that Robert started.

Mildred wanted to live.

# SYMON

He wasn't entirely sure what he would do until he was already doing it.

Symon was not a strategist; he was an animal that sometimes walked in the body of a man. The beast in him, a snarling creature that had only grown stronger since his embrace, howled into the emptiness of his mind.

If Symon heeded the desire of the monster within him, then he would tear Burghley House apart and leave all but Mildred as nothing more than mutilated scraps of flesh and fabric.

But that would not win the love of his mate, which even his beast longed for. Symon struck an accord, his rational mind holding back the violent cascade his soul wished to unleash on anyone between him and his red-haired strawberry.

The stink of poison wafted through his senses as he moved through the darkness of the long hall. It mingled with Mildred's scent so closely that for a moment he feared she had consumed it.

Lord Burghley stepped into the darkness in front of him. The willow lights were dim, leaving plenty of dark nooks for Symon to hide in, but the man moved with a sure step that belied his absolute mastery of his domain.

He would not be so secure any longer.

Symon's wrath was hot and quick, and Lord Burghley found himself hauled up by the decadent fabric of his doublet, a hunk of the man's beard tangled in Symon's hand, yanking at the lord's pride as the vampire raised an arm and delivered a sharp blow with the back of his hand.

He wouldn't give the lord the dignity of a punch, not when a lazy slap bruised the doughy nobleman in his grip so readily.

It happened too quickly, faster than his self control, which was a shame. Symon had a speech prepared and everything. He intended to emasculate the lord, but he would have to settle for the look of raw prey panic on the human's face as he threw him into the door he'd just exited from.

The firelight from the room cast Symon in deep, red shadow as he stepped into the library with the weak willow light haloing his dark form like an avenging angel.

Tears stained his mate's beautiful face as she held her son against her, trying to shield the boy from the sight of his mangled, but living, father. For a moment, he wondered if her terror was true, but their eyes locked and he saw the flash of relief in those mossy green eyes.

He could sense her emotions through their bond now that he drew closer to her. The fear was present, but so was relief and longing.

"Please — don't hurt him."

Rage coursed through Symon as he considered she might mean her former husband, beaten but breathing behind them. Terra Noxa's most ancient laws dissolved their marriage bonds, and he couldn't fathom why she would beg for the life of a man who would have poisoned her.

One of the boy's sobs cut through Symon's haze, and he realized that she was afraid for her son, that fear crystallized between them as he closed the distance and gripped her wrist.

Never.

He tried to push that feeling through their bond, that he would never intentionally harm her child, but the lord groaned atop his pile of wood, and Symon knew they had to move quickly from this place.

If he stayed a moment longer, he would kill Elizabeth Tudor's favorite pet, and that would bring complications his people were not ready to deal with just yet.

Symon pulled Mildred into the hall, allowing her to turn one last time to reach out to her son and shout into the still room.

"I love you!"

It was not wise to carry a mortal while running at full speed, but something followed at their heels. A keen, dead thing that croaked and flew like a raven soared above them. He recognized the unnatural creature and steeled himself against the urge to recoil at the necromancer's pet.

Even an unnatural, demonically quick bird couldn't keep pace with a vampire running at full tilt into the dense forest, and the creature soon veered off back toward the manor. If the boy was skilled, he might have seen through the creature's eyes and spied the direction they ran.

There was every chance that Mildred's son understood more than either of them wanted him to, but Symon could do nothing about it now. For the time being, he would keep that knowledge to himself.

It would do nothing but push his mate into further turmoil, and he had terrorized her enough that evening. For the first time since their bond had formed the night before, he had to force the connection to muffle between them, but he hoped it would only be temporary.

It was not a good thing to begin their life with a falsehood between them.

# MILDRED

Her lover carried her like a new bride through the forest and ran so quickly that the cold autumn air stung her cheeks and it was difficult to take in a full breath. Mildred curled against his neck and made herself as small as possible as the night melted around them. She didn't know where he was taking her, but she didn't care.

She was numb to everything but the receding presence of the old stones beneath Burghley House and the last moment with Robert. His red-rimmed eyes and terror-stricken tears would haunt her for the rest of her existence.

That strange, cold, despairing numbness dissipated almost as quickly as it came on as foreign emotions seeped into her psyche. Guilt and determination poured from Symon as he carried her through the darkness, though she sensed he was hiding something from her.

Mildred was too weary to press him on it.

Time passed, an hour, perhaps two, and they came upon a rocky strip of shoreline. He must have run several miles to have reached the sea. It was a full day's ride on horse to the nearest port and longer than that on foot through wild lands.

A dark shape bobbed far out on the surf, where the water was deep enough to hide a sizable merchant ship. The young vampire from her flight with Ness three days earlier stood in the waves, water lapping up to his knees with a rowboat by his side.

"I was about to abandon you for dead, Lupou," the other vampire, Stefan, said with a smile. Then he turned his head toward Mildred and bowed. It was ridiculous with the cold water swirling around them as Symon stepped toward the waves, and she let out a manic peal of laughter.

"You again," was all Mildred could bring herself to say.

"Yes, my lady," Stefan said with an air of wistfulness. "I am happy to see you well. I do hope this brute has treated you kindly." Stefan's voice grew serious as he looked her over, but Symon responded with a growl.

"My mate is well. You'll watch where you lay your eyes," Symon hefted her onto the boat so that not a drop of the frigid channel water soaked into her gown.

The two vampires joined her, each taking an oar and rowing them out toward the boat with a dizzying swiftness that made her head ache if she stared too long at the blurred movement of their arms.

Instead, she watched the shoreline receding as a pale sliver of the moon cast a silver mantle of light over the rocky shores of England.

"Will I ever see it again?" she whispered to herself, one hand gripping her silver pomander and the other pressing against her breast where her heart beat with frightening speed.

"I promise you will, and we will much improve it upon our return, my love," Symon said cryptically.

It could only mean that soon England would suffer the same fate as the Holy Roman Empire and Italy.

"Perhaps they will improve themselves." She thought of

Robert and all the choices that lay before him. Symon was right: her sacrifice could not save his soul; only he could do that for himself.

She prayed one day Robert would come to understand her own choices, and they could face the repercussions of them together.

Those prayers were as good as smoke, though, because echoing against the crashing waves, and above the sound of the rowboat slamming into the ship's side, she heard the low, laughing croak of a dead raven.

# ABOUT THE AUTHOR

Augusta Grey collects books, cats, and fountain pens. She can be found in the Pacific Northwest, where she enjoys lazy hikes, hot cups of tea and reading on the couch with her fae spouse.

Want free bonus scenes and updates on new publications? Join Augusta Grey's mailing list.

subscribepage.io/VSxjLo

If you enjoyed The Black Wolf and the Red Hare, please consider leaving a review and following on Amazon or social media.

Tiktok : @augustagreytheauthor

Instagram : https://www.instagram.com/augustagreyauthor/

# BACKMATTER

## ACKNOWLEDGMENTS

I am a trash-goblin by nature and would get nothing done without the not-so-gentle prodding from my friends and family. The world of Terra Noxa has unfolded over cups of tea and brunch for four years, and I wouldn't have pushed through to make this book a reality without my loved ones to soak up all the lore stored up in my head.

Thank you, Davey. My partner in crime, you always aid and abet my hair-brained schemes.

To Amber, for editing, moral support, and Kpop breaks.

To Sophie and Jesse, for writing sprints and accountability. I am your first and biggest fan.

To Mom and Dad, dear Gods, please don't read this book.

To the Weavers, the hearth of my heart.

To Haleigh, my first beta reader and the one who made this book feel real.

To Arlo, who helped birth Augusta Grey and gave her a coat of arms.

www.ingramcontent.com/pod-product-compliance
Lightning Source LLC
LaVergne TN
LVHW011030110826
845149LV00015B/3362